STAY

THE CURSED GODS SERIES

JENNIFER SILVERWOOD

Copyright 2020 Jennifer Silverwood

Edited by
Red Adept Editing

Developmental Editor
RJ Locksley

Cover Art and Interior Formatting by
Qamber Designs & Media

License Notes
All rights reserved including the right to produce this novel and/or portions of it without specific permission from the author. This novel is a work of fiction. All names, characters, incidents and places are purely fictitious. As much of this was derived deep within the mad musings of an authoress, that should be obvious.

"Sometimes love isn't as magical as people expect it to be."
— CLAUDIA

1

THE NEW COUPLE

is scent was my undoing, because he didn't smell like sweat and grime or the spices some men used to mask their odor. He smelled like the skies before a rain and the sea air as it wafts into the harbor.

His lips brushed against my ear as he gently lifted my hair to expose my neck. A gust of wind chilled my skin, and I shivered beneath the heat of his touch.

"Orona…I wish you would let me love you."

"Never," I whispered and watched his eyes spark with brewing tempests. The skies blackened with his mood and crackled as the waves crashed harder against the nearby rocks. Yet even in the force of the oncoming gale, I clenched my fists and stood firm.

It was for this reason he first fell in love with me.

For two thousand years, I had walked this earth, cursed with the compulsion to test true love. I became the angel of judgment, the precursor to their heartache and pain, the grace of another woman's lips on his collar, the scent of her perfume on his skin…I had arranged all these to afflict and to tempt. For it was easy to love while untried and pure. Forgiveness for some people came at too high a price, and trust was not easily won.

Once, a simple look was enough. I could look at them and *know* in my heart they would last, that they would spend the rest of their lives together. Yet that was a time when men protected their women, not because they were property, but because they loved.

Not like this new world where women are too strong to let men care for them. Not this cruel world where women die alone and unloved because they have forgotten how to trust. When they forgot how to trust, men forgot how to remember their strength. And I have watched this old world forget its first love, to forget itself in a search for something and everything meaningless.

They forgot that true love is worth fighting for above all things.

I had watched empires rise and fall, disease and famine sweep over the earth. Love remained the same, only now it was much rarer. Now they tried to paint it with different colors, sex and lust, obsession. But all these were only illusions for the truth.

Pictures of barely clothed women flashed across on skyscraper walls. Songs played from an endless sea of boxes and speakers across the city. On my rare off days, I could almost stand to listen and learn how much the world had changed.

I heard them now as I walked through the city streets in my cloak. After a thousand years, my clothes had fallen out of fashion.

And I had grown so used to my tunic and sandals, I had no care to keep up with men's fickle taste. If I were truly honest, I had not altered my appearance in two thousand years for one shameful reason. I wanted *him* to look down on me and remember.

A lesser reason might be the fact I was no longer human. Cursed immortality would do that to anyone like me. I no longer felt cold or heat, no longer the silky feel of the dress *he* had given me brush against my bare skin. And when I wore my cloak, I was only a blur at the edge of their vision, gooseflesh on their skin. People walked through me and blamed it on their imagination.

Another side effect of man's downfall was they had also forgotten to trust that still-small voice in their heads. The one that assured them there was no scientific explanation for unexplained phenomenon. My very existence defied all their explanations.

The city was beautiful and wicked, but it was a false beauty compared to the things I had seen. When he cursed me, I could feel *everything*, from contentment to sorrow, but never love. He had given me the ability to see it in others and destroy it when it was false or save it if true. Yet the only thing that managed to stir me these days was the memory of my death. Only my memories kept me going. Vengefully I often wished he still knew my every thought and suffered the recall of our every moment together.

Thinking of Seid made my cloak slip enough to expose an outline of my features. I never would have noticed my mistake if the dark-skinned boy coming my way hadn't pointed and began to shout a stream of curses to his friends. Other people were turning and beginning to take notice—the old couple clutching onto each other to ward away the winter chill, the little girl picking their pocket for loose change, black-market vendors dealing on the side.

Breathing in deeply, an ancient but unnecessary habit now, I drew the fabric tighter and focused on my mission. For several minutes, I ran faster than their eyes could follow, beating myself on the inside for my carelessness.

"You must never be seen by anyone," his words echoed in my memories, settled deep in my bones, and made me shiver. I couldn't think about Seid now, not when I needed to focus.

My new mission was close. When I turned the colors in my eyes just right, I could see his aura through the chaos of buildings and people. And the closer I drifted, the faster I was, until I was no longer walking but floating, flying through every obstacle in my path.

Looking up at the buildings, I noticed the flashing lights had been mercifully left behind. Once his building was in sight, my pulse began to sputter, to race and soar. I could feel the budding newness of his affection for her in my chest and savored it. This is the closest I came to feeling human emotions these days.

My vision cleared once I stood outside the window before them. All sound ceased to exist, save their words and breaths. The café was dimly lit, a very old nightclub from the looks of it. Wordless music crooned up from below, horns and the strokes of piano keys. Feet shuffled in rhythm to the soft beat of a drum.

That was when I heard their voices for the first time.

"You look so perfect tonight, Lissa…" he practically growled in her ear.

She giggled and answered in a sultry tone, "Good enough to eat?"

Chuckling low, he kissed her on the lips, "That's right, baby."

I frowned as the brick wall kept blocking my vision and realized too late I wasn't peering through a window. I would have to go inside to better see. Walking through walls used to scare me senseless, until I grew accustomed to it. Now I brushed the feeling aside as I squeezed past the gritty matter. The front room was built to disguise the underground world beneath it. Worn down like the rest of this city, no one would ever believe the cultural haven it sheltered.

For a brief moment, I recalled brilliant jewels and brassy music, short dresses lined with tassels of an era gone by, and women's laughter over the clink of glasses of forbidden liquid.

The newest incarnation pulled me back to the present. I had passed through the secret door, walked down a short flight of stairs, and now watched from inside the smoky club. Here women still dressed to please, and men of a higher class sought their nightly trophies. On stage, the jazz band played, and at the center of the dance floor, my newest assignment drank their fill of each other.

When the tempo began to drag into a slower tune, she tilted her head back to expose her neck. Her long brown locks trailed to her red-clad hips. He tightened his hold on her waist as he kissed her neck. And I could feel the thrill in her heart temporarily mask a quiet sorrow.

Yet there was nothing from the man.

I frowned and turned my eyes to the rest of the establishment. Where was the budding newness of his affection I so strongly felt outside?

"Excuse me?" A deep, rough voice came from behind me, over my shoulder, and I froze.

He cannot see me.

Convinced that he was speaking to another patron, I nearly walked on. Perhaps I was not close enough to them to feel the man's love for this girl?

"Come back to my place…" I clearly heard the man whisper into the woman's ear. Her emerald eyes sparkled as she batted her lashes and pulled back her full lips in a saucy grin.

I shook my head. Sex was never the key to a man's unwavering devotion. Yet she was considering it, hoping it would give him reason enough to keep her around longer, *this* time. I paused as a flurry of images and sensations flashed past behind my eyes. It took some time, depending on the difficulty of my mission, to grow accustomed to their emotions. Rather than simple feeling, human emotions often carried scattered memories and impressions. I pushed the usual discomfort aside.

I took another step and gasped when a hard hand clasped my shoulder and spun me firmly round.

Impossible…

No one touched me, had not in two thousand years.

Yet his hand remained planted on my shoulder in its firm grip, and I followed the shape of his muscled arm to the chest attached to it. His black shirt was a tight fit and, in the dim blue and red lights, seemed to flash several colors. He bent down so his eyes met my line of sight.

My mouth dropped the moment I breathed in his scent.

He smells like the skies before a rain and the sea air as it wafts into the harbor…

My vision blackened and suddenly broke through in brilliant flashes of light around his face. I could feel the colors growing, shifting and glowing in my eyes, beneath my skin. I clenched my fists as I fought for control, convinced I had lost it for the first time. Had I wanted him so badly in my memories that they came to life?

Reaching up to clutch my waist, he kept me from falling down the short flight of stairs. A frown creased his brow as he said, "Whoa there, take it easy. I didn't mean to scare you. It's just my job to check everyone before they come in. You got any ID?"

I shook my head slowly and watched as those eyes, *his* eyes, shifted from the dance floor and back to me a few times. Holding up a couple of fingers, he nodded to someone over my shoulder and returned his attention to me. Something akin to recognition flickered in those dark-blue eyes. Clenching his firm jaw, he sighed and then nodded to himself.

"Look, miss," he began, "I'm really sorry, but you can't stay here without any ID. Any chance you can find your way back up?"

I was trembling. Just hearing his voice again set every forgotten nerve in my body on edge. My flesh was on fire beneath my cloak where his fingers touched. Still, I had forgotten my voice for too long and could not remember how to speak.

My cloak.

How could he see me when I had refastened my cloak once again? It was such a thin, flimsy thing, like a second skin I wore so often I forgot about it. But no human had ever seen me beneath it before.

It has to be him.

His frown deepened, and his voice dropped to a softer, unused tone. "You're shaking all over… You okay?"

No one else has the power to see.

My mouth opened, but no sound came out. I was forbidden to speak to the humans. And even though he had Seid's face, the curse commanded my attention. Oddly enough, I could feel what he felt.

He feels nothing toward me.

He did not recognize me.

His eyes flickered up as two pairs of feet approached us from behind. Immediately, his arm curled me closer to his chest, and his eyes darkened.

Lissa and her date were speaking in hushed tones, but I heard them as clear as the true light.

"—so hard you'll see stars," the man was saying.

Lissa giggled and playfully swatted him with her clutch. "Derek!"

They paused on our level at the head of the stair. Another girl brought their jackets to them. As Derek helped Lissa into her fur jacket, her gaze locked onto the man holding me.

That was when the truth settled over me with horrifying clarity. The aura I had followed across a country, across a city, was burning brightly between them. Invisible to them, the golden strands were weak now, but the link between them unmistakable. It linked this man, the man who wore *his face*, to her, Lissa.

The man holding me tensed and clutched me tighter to him again, his words stuck on the roof of his mouth.

Instead, the other girl who handed out and hung cloaks offered, "Good job tonight. See you tomorrow, Lissa," as Derek and Lissa walked through the secret door.

And to my horror, I watched the threads that linked them to me stretch and fade.

"We just clicked instantly. I knew we were two pieces to a whole."
— ANDREA

"We just clicked instantly. I knew we were two pieces to a whole."
— ANDREA

2

Ties that Bind

His chest heaved and brushed against my arm, eliciting prickles of feeling up my spine. My heart was being carved out of my chest all over again, and I had not even begun to test them yet. Rather, I felt I was the one being tested.

What sort of cruel punishment is this?

I wanted to cry out to the gathering storm clouds the humans were oblivious to. Winds were shifting from the north, clouds gathering into a thick blanket filled with promise. A blizzard was coming, the first to strike this city in some time. But things were changing constantly in man's world. When they forgot how to love, they lost the will to care for their fragile earth. Now things were shifting again, a sign of my hopelessness, a sign of the growing darkness. And in my heart of hearts, I knew I was failing in my task.

Cloak girl was speaking to *him* now, their voices distant and dreamlike to my ears. I was pulled back to the present the moment his grip eased and slipped lower to gently clasp my waist.

"Some suit, eh? How much you think that guy brings in a year? Gotta be at least fifty times all our salaries combined." The pretty dark-skinned girl turned her head and chewed her gum thoughtfully. "And Lissa's gonna get a mouthful from the boss for leaving before her last number. Betcha he fires her tight little..."

"Chloe..." he growled in warning.

Shrugging, she twisted the tie around her neck as though it were too tight. "Sorry, Cain, but I call 'em like I see 'em. I'm just sayin'..."

Cain answered so low the girl couldn't have possibly caught the brokenness hidden within his words. "You've said enough."

I wondered why the girl had yet to notice me. If this man could see me, what was to stop everyone else? I latched onto a glimmer of hope.

Perhaps it was a mistake, a glitch.

The cloak *was* two thousand years old, after all. Seid had fashioned it to protect my form from the rare human that chanced having *the sight*. And I had long ago stopped caring whether the curse kept me from their clueless eyes.

I held my breath and tried to slip out of his grip.

Cain's blue eyes turned stormy gray, instantly zeroing in on me as he remembered what he held in his hands. In the blink of an eye, I shared the remnants of the anger and frustration he felt for the woman in the red dress, his Lissa. From what I had seen, there seemed to be little love lost between them.

Had the world fallen so far that this was the best couple he could find me?

He finally spoke, eyes peering into the darkness of my hood. "Sorry…forgot about you there for a sec." Cain paused when I gave no answer and frowned, conflicted over the wild feelings clouding his aura. "So…no ID, huh? Were you meeting someone here?"

Ignoring him, I looked through the walls of this building and watched Lissa and Derek exchanging kisses in between steps to his parked limo. The man followed my gaze to the brick wall, and an amused grimace troubled his handsome face.

I couldn't read minds. No, that was a gift Seid had used over weaker souls than my own. But the feelings of passionate humans often carried pictures and color with them. From these I could sense this man's sudden loneliness, his anger and a deeper pain.

In all this time, I had never come upon two souls already so thoroughly lost.

But perhaps I judged them too quickly?

When I turned back my attention, I was once again struck by Cain's familiarity. Even the resonance of his voice was the same when he spoke.

An unwanted anxiousness settled in the pit of my abdomen, the ache I had felt since the moment Seid cursed me. At times I hated myself for missing him after everything he had done to me.

"Look, miss, I'm trying to help you out here. But you have to give me a name to go on." Something flickered in and out of his gaze again, as though he too was trying to place my face from his memories, but then it was gone.

Shaking my head at my ridiculous thoughts, I tried to pry from his grasp and frowned when I did not budge. It had been so long since I felt this *fleshy* that it frightened me. No walls were too thick for me to pass through, no waves powerful enough to crush me. I was used to feeling invincible. My efforts to escape surprised him. Cain laughed as I struggled in vain to escape while his arms barely strained.

"Easy there. You're not in trouble, okay? But this is an exclusive club, and the boss don't like me letting in charity cases."

Cain's grip eased when I stilled. For a long, tense moment, we stared back at one another. His eyes were beautiful in the false lights, and in the center of his black pupils, I saw my reflection, my own eyes faintly glowing in the shadow of my cloak.

To show him I agreed, I nodded my head after another beat. The left corner of his mouth lifted higher when he grinned, because of the strange scar on his cheek. This new feature startled and drew my gaze. My love had been perfection in every way, save his rotten core.

When I moved to leave this time, he let go of my waist, but his eyes followed. A different emotion hung over him now, obscured to me and troubling. I could not bear to look away as I faded into the shadows. With an easy shove, Cain opened the secret door and left it open long after I had passed through.

The further I drew apart from him, the stronger the compulsion grew within me to turn back, the brighter the aura glowed around him.

Chloe laughed then. "Geez man! Who you waiting for? There's nobody there, and you're lettin' the draft in."

He turned to challenge her. From this distance, I could see the giant of a man he truly was. "You didn't see that woman? Come on, she was just here, Chloe."

"Who? I ain't seen nobody leave 'cept the ho who left you

high and dry."

"Chloe…" He groaned into his hand, but when he turned to find me, I had already faded through to the other side.

Something was wrong. The wall had almost refused to budge when I first pressed against it, and the strain as I fell through left me in shivers. Snow had begun to seriously rain from the dark clouds above the city. Horns blared in the distance, tires skidding on a collective layer of ice.

I checked my cloak once more to be certain it was secure and breathed a sigh of relief. Except this time, the air escaping my lips appeared in a wet, puffy cloud of heat. I frowned and sank against the side of the building, confused and not wanting to think that I might be lost.

Had I done something wrong? There was no other explanation why I had already so obviously failed my mission. Perhaps if I followed the golden thread of a trail Lissa left behind? But why had she chosen Derek over Cain? Usually the lovers were together when I came to them, often living in the same place.

I was usually called to them at their most critical time together, the final test and the last chance.

Yet instead of following Lissa, I listened to the pull of the man in the club. The music ended abruptly, and a smooth male voice followed. "Weather's turning nasty out there, ladies and gents. We've been advised to send all y'all on your way. But don't fret, don't stress, more music to be had this following Saturday."

Voices rose up, and drinks tipped back for a final swig. Servers rushed to clean while their guests moved to the secret door. I watched as fancy cars and limos waited to pick up their important clients. A flurry of the fancy and trashy paraded past my eyes, but I cared little. Too much focus right now gave my head a spin. I could see the heartache and trouble that filled their lives, and knew why they had all come this night.

Time often passed me in leaps and jumps. I do not know how long I sat there, pressed against the building after the last car had gone. The sky had shifted color, however, behind that thick veil of gray to a hidden dawn. Still I rested deep in my memories, the closest I could come to dreaming.

Despair was the color of my nightmares. I realized then that I was still shivering, and the recognition hit me with a cloud of terror. I could *feel* the cold. Staring at the vacant street in a numb shock, I was too afraid to ponder why.

⦿⦿⦿

Chloe called to him before he walked out, "Don't be jealous 'cause the boss likes my breasts and not yours." She laughed loudly.

"Last chance to catch a ride with me, Chloe."

"And chance being stuck with *you* for more than ten hours? In your dreams, big guy. Later!"

My skin tingled the nearer he came and burned with an inner fire once Cain stepped out the front door into the storm. Snow had caked my cloak with a fine layer of white dust. Had I not lived at the edge of the emerald sea in my human years, I would have thought to be afraid.

From the safety of my hood, I took him in. He was coated by a heavy leather jacket, a skin-tight woolen cap, scarf, and gloves he was currently blowing warmth into. Shaking out his limbs in a way that was entirely too familiar, Cain turned his head and froze. I flinched when his gaze found mine. How could he see through my cloak again? I should compel him to look away, but I didn't *want* him to look away.

Gather your senses!

While I struggled to find my sanity, Cain drew closer and startled me by the sound of his voice. "Miss? What are you still doing out here?" Glancing down the street, he shook his head. I could feel his frustration. "You know it's already twenty below? You're gonna freeze if we don't get you home."

Tilting my chin up to meet him, I felt the snow graze my bare skin and gasped at the sensation. I pushed my cloak aside and held my bare arm out to feel the wind slide through my fingers.

"Are you wearing anything underneath that cloak of yours?" he asked. When I didn't answer, he grasped his head in his hands and let them slide down his cheeks with a frustrated groan.

I kept my hand outstretched and spoke, my voice raspy with disuse. "Can you feel it? It's so cold."

"She speaks after all," he said with wide eyes. His smile turned inward and tugged one corner of his mouth into an upturned grin. "Yes, it's cold—damned cold—meaning you'll freeze to death if we don't get you some shelter."

Something in his words surged inside of me and gave me the energy to stand. Before I could take another step, he was there, clutching me around the waist and helping me out of the drift. I turned and found the stubble on his strong jaw with my fingertips and smiled.

Cain's jaw slackened, and he blinked rapidly before finding his voice again. "Can I help you get a cab at least?" He sounded doubtful, as though he already knew I had nowhere to go but with him.

Certainty claimed my conscience at the thought.

This is the answer, to go with him.

He pushed me back by the shoulders so he could look me in the eye and offered another grin. "Guess that's a no, huh?" His brow furrowed when I shivered. "You're freezing…" His hands moved to pull mine from my cloak and began to rub them down.

His warmth sank through his gloves and into my skin. There was a moment when our eyes met and he seemed to question his actions. Confusion was pushed aside by determination in the end. In him I saw for the briefest of moments, for the first time in a century, the strength of men.

"I'm Cain, by the way."

He paused after but didn't press for my name. I watched him fight the war within himself. Would he leave me here? Could I even follow him now I was beginning to feel again? My eyes fell to our joined hands, where his thumb brushed slow circles over my upturned palms. My shiver came not from the cold then.

"So," he began, almost nervously, "I don't normally do this, but…would you want to come with me? My place ain't much, but it's warmer than this."

I smiled at this impossible human and said, "Yes."

"He would literally do anything for me…"
—RUTH

3

To Breathe, To Feel

Cain drove a battered old motorcycle, the sort that spoke of journeys taken and better years gone by. After settling me in behind him, we flew. I had never ridden in a car, train, or boat unless absolutely necessary. Never before had the wind stung my cheeks with the cold bite of sleet.

Chains kept his tires from skidding over the ice, and the same power I had noticed in his every movement manifested here. Pressed against him with my arms around his waist, I could no longer feel the cold.

Home for this human was a flat among dozens in a rundown old neighborhood. Allowing my senses to stretch farther, I could easily feel the pain and heartache in most. Happiness and love were nearly nonexistent.

He parked and locked his bike next to a row of others, lifting me easily to stand ankle deep in snow. His arm sheltered me up the walk, to the first of many steps to his home. I gasped when my legs buckled and threatened to give out, bracing my hand on the gritty rail. Without another word, Cain swept me up in his arms and carried me the rest of the way.

Human life was a messy, noisy din around us, but I had learned long ago to drown most of it out.

Cain glanced down at me briefly before plugging his keys into the lock. "Sorry my place ain't much to look at."

A single dim glow came from a nearby glass case. After flipping on the lights, he turned and shut the door with one hand, bracing me to him with the other.

I wrapped my arms about his neck and rested my forehead on his chest. For one stolen moment, I imagined I was human again, my curse broken. But the compulsion of my new mission fell like a brass weight about my neck. Behind my closed lids, I could still see Lissa's emerald eyes as she stole a final glance at Cain. I remembered his longing for her.

"Sorry 'bout the mess," he said as his chest vibrated beneath my face. "Wasn't expecting company."

Turning my head back to the apartment, I watched him sweep aside a stack of papers before he set me to rest on an old couch. His home was small and sparse. An antique table sat in front of the couch, covered with more papers, books, and empty cans. Metal weights were piled in one corner of his living room. Past this was something I had not thought to see again. The stereo was long and tall, and the turntable open and ready for a fresh record.

When I turned to search for the kitchen, my eyes met a pair of long, jean-clad legs and traveled up their length to his belt and tucked-in black shirt. Cain popped his knuckles repeatedly into his palm, watching me watch him. Again I could feel his nervousness through the link that connected him and Lissa to me.

Keeping my head bowed low, I noticed he had already pulled off his leather jacket and scarf.

Cain tugged the cap roughly off his short-cropped inky-black hair and began wringing it in his hands. "So…" he began, clearing his throat as he attempted a smile. "I was thinking I could pull out the couch for you tonight. It's already got sheets on it, can't promise how fresh though." Shifting on his feet again, he peered into the depths of my cloak and waited for an answer.

"Yes," I replied. I could hear my accent despite the rasp of my throat when I spoke. It summoned distant memories of a language and people long dead, of boats and fish and the sweet salty sea.

Cain nodded to himself and glanced at the howling storm careening outside his window. "Looks like it's gonna be real bad this time. They say we haven't had a winter like this in years."

"I know."

"Well," he said after an awkward pause, "don't worry. I already stocked up on supplies, so we should be good if it decides to hold out. Do you, ah, wanna borrow one of my sweaters?" He gestured to the silvery-blue skirts peeking from beneath my gray cloak.

"Thank you," I replied, though I was not sure it was a wise decision, since I already felt so off balance.

With a thoughtful smile on his lips, Cain nodded and disappeared through another door. From the flats around us, babies screamed, couples fought and screamed threats, and others held silent in fear of the coming storm.

I removed my cloak and carefully folded it until it easily slid into the pocket of my tunic. Gooseflesh rose on my arms as the chilled air rested on my skin. Cain had been right; it was cold, but not like the city beyond his window.

"Here you—" Cain's confidence faded to a whisper, "go..."

I turned at the sound of his voice, my waist-length curls shifting in spite of the many intricate braids I had woven them into. Our eyes met and seemed to come together in a force as swift as the tide. Cain's jaw clenched then released as he drew in a desperate breath, as though he'd only just come up for air again.

I closed the space between us. "Thank you."

Our fingers brushed as he handed over the heavy wool. I watched his pupil overcome the iris, only to once more be consumed by rich indigo.

"Added some sweats and socks, since our building's boiler is shit," he offered. "Sorry I can't offer you more, but this should keep you warm, at least." Shoving his hands in his pockets, he glared at the floor. "You can change in my bathroom. It's through that door and on the right."

I listened to the pounding of his heart as I passed.

෨෨෨

Cain's bedroom was dark but much more like a home than the rest of his flat. The bed took up most of the space.

I smiled to myself.

Anything smaller, and he'd have to curl into a ball.

The bathroom light was already on. I looked at the razor and scattered dark hairs in the sink. Beside a sweet-smelling tube sat a toothbrush still in its package.

I lifted my eyes and found my reflection. Rare it was that I even glimpsed my face. So often I lived in that in-between place of shadows and light. I frowned at the creature before me and realized I could not remember the last time I had met this woman in the mirror.

Silver threads wove through curling golden hair and hung over an ancient tunic. In my human life, those wheat tresses had been the envy of every girl in the village, a rarity that made me stand apart. *His* symbol still covered the clasp that held my dress together. My features were sharp and angular yet surprisingly soft. Clan markings decorated the sides of my neck, signs of an age gone by. My skin was sun-kissed, the same deep olive of my people. Until the need to protect or destroy overcame me, it would remain untouched by color and light. For now, the gift rested within my eyes, glowing with flecks of every shade, the eyes of a cursed god.

Grimacing, I turned away from my reflection, fisted the silver clasp, and held my breath as I removed it.

I cannot say what Cain felt when I emerged from his room, but the full weight of his emotions hit me like a breaking wave on the rocks. The neck of his sweater was so big on my narrow frame, it fell over my shoulder. I hadn't bothered with the too-large pants in favor of rolling the socks up my calves. The sweater's edge brushed my hips, and I clutched hold of the wool with my fists as I met his unsettled gaze.

Light emanated from the kitchen space behind Cain and obscured his features with shadows. Again came the crack and pop of his knuckles in his palm.

"Is this acceptable?" I whispered.

"Oh yeah—I mean, yeah." Cain rubbed a hand over his face and turned his head toward the crackle of his stereo. "I hope the pullout is okay with you," he said, gesturing to the expanded couch behind me.

I gasped as I turned and bent to run my hands over the sheets, then glanced over my shoulder to ask, "How did you perform this magic?"

Cain shifted on his feet in what I was learning to be a nervous gesture, and I wondered if he meant to join me. Something held him back, however.

Laughter clung to his voice as he replied, "Never thought of it as magic, really. But good to know you're easily pleased..." He froze, regret seeping through our connection, and rubbed a hand over his short-cropped hair.

I smiled as I sank down on the magical bed and watched him, transfixed in spite of myself. Never had silence disturbed me before this, yet nothing compared to the heaviness in the air or the tension stewing in my limbs. I was fascinated by the rapid beat of his heart within his sculpted chest, a syncopated beat for my ears alone.

Cain swayed slightly forward and then released a bated breath. "Well. I'll let you get settled in then. Just—let me know if you need anything, okay?" When he stepped fully into the light,

I could see that the scar on his cheek extended down further into his chin and past his neck. "Okay…" he assured himself and forced a troubled smile before he softly said, "goodnight."

"I wouldn't take back a single moment we spent together, because within that wild rocky roller coaster ride…I truly believe I did experience love."
— CHELSEA

4

WAITING FOR THE STORM

When I first saw him, I vowed never to love another man again. The man Father arranged for me to marry beat me with his fists when I refused to pleasure him, the night of the feast. He was not to touch me until the contracts had been inscribed, but he claimed he could not wait. This man was too powerful, and when father refused to see my bruises, I ran away.

The sea was my first home. With all I possessed, I ran to the end of the village, the farthest tip of land jutting out into the emerald sea. This place had been my retreat since childhood. If I could only gather my thoughts and think of a plan before stealing aboard a frigate like a madwoman, I might have a chance. Now that I had nowhere else to go, this was the last place I felt safe.

A stranger was waiting for me. His eyes were what first struck me, so unnatural and blue, the shade of every sky and storm. I loved him first then, though I refused to know it…

Night and day had no meaning in the eye of the storm, yet I woke from dreaming when the sun rose over the horizon. I looked past the endless rows of flats above his through the discolored ceiling, above the sea of white masking the glorious dawn. I loved the dawn as much as I had loved the sea in my youth. The morning I met Seid, I believed the sun had brought him to me.

Pushing aside the old quilt, I clutched my heart and gasped an unnecessary breath at the realization.

I slept…

Fear creased the hidden lines in my brow. What had I done? What had changed? And then the slightest tweak of hope awoke like the dawn in my chest.

Is the curse weakening?

Cain stirred in his bed, sheets rustling as he spoke in his sleep. Jerking my head to peer through the thin wall separating us, I was relieved to find him yet asleep. My eyes lingered on the outline of his frame as an old longing rose up.

No.

I grasped my head with my hands so my hair created a curtain around my vision. I had dreamed for the first time in centuries. And all my dreams had been of *him*, of course. I could never escape him, he had sworn in his fury.

"Lost to all mortal boundaries, forever you shall be my Orona…"

"You're already awake, huh?" Cain's voice was rough from sleep.

I jumped, startled to hear Seid's voice coming from so different, yet so similar a man, and stared owlishly up at how he filled the doorframe.

Cain chuckled. "Sorry, didn't mean to scare you. But you did say I was magic, remember?" His eyes gleamed brighter until they borrowed the shade of the morning sky. "Did you sleep okay? If you hate the couch, I can give you the bed, now that I know you won't kill me in my sleep." His smirk faded when I continued to blankly stare. His eyes wandered, and confusion clouded his aura. The tight mask I had seen him wear over his expression the night before was back in place when he turned.

Gathering my legs up from beneath me, I rested my chin on my knees. "It was fine."

"Good," he said, though I could tell his thoughts were far away as he walked past the bar and into his kitchen. Besides his dark sweats and socks, Cain wore a skintight sleeveless shirt over his bare chest. The latter was solely for my benefit, I sensed, so he did not embarrass me. Like most men I had observed, the less clothing he wore to sleep, the better.

I could sense everything he was feeling as he began sifting through cupboards and drawers. He was distracted by something and frustrated even more by something else. An underlying ache had remained with him ever since our eyes first linked. And had he not been my mission, had I not seen him look at Lissa, I might have wondered if that ache was for me.

Cain slapped his palms on his countertop and leaned forward with a sheepish grin. "So…I don't stock up on normal stuff. Wasn't expecting you, so I don't know if you'll like my cooking or not. It's an acquired taste."

"I do not eat," I answered with a shrug and not for a second worrying how mad that would sound.

His eyes widened. "Um…okay then. Guess that takes care

of *that* problem." Chuckling to himself, he rubbed the back of his neck and shook his head.

The truth was I had not required a single meal in two thousand years. At least I held enough sense to keep this additional detail from the human.

Cain did not feel it necessary to fill the silence with useless words, something I was grateful for. I watched him cook and eat his food for a time and wondered what the taste would be like to me now. In my time, the fruit from my mother's garden would have filled my belly. The substance he shoveled into his mouth hardly looked like food to me.

He frowned through his breakfast, an expression that turned into a grimace while he washed his bowl and set it out to dry. By the time Cain finished, I could feel the determination rolling off of him in waves as he crossed the room. His eyes lingered everywhere else in the room but me, though I sensed he desperately wanted to do otherwise. Crossing his impressive arms over his chest, he attempted to break the ice.

"So, I didn't ask you last night because you looked like you needed the handout. But seeing as we're stuck here together till this storm breaks, I figure we need to talk through a few things."

"Yes."

His eyes flicked up suddenly and roamed my face then, lingered on the curl of my tresses resting along my back and trailing over the magic bed. His brown skin burned a deeper, almost rusty shade. After taking in another breath, he shut his eyes. "Yes, you agree? Or yes, you're just saying that because you don't know much English?"

"I know English," I said, though my accent certainly made

his question valid.

He opened his cerulean eyes, and his smile tugged at the scar on his cheek. "Okay, that answers that question. So, if you're not hiding from the law, what were you doing at the club last night?" His gaze traveled from the braids that tied my hair out of my face to the tattoos that trailed past the neck of his sweater.

I smiled and debated how much I could safely say. Usually, the humans I helped would forget me after. Cain seemed to break those rules.

"I have a job to do," I tentatively began, "but I am afraid I already failed."

His eyes narrowed on the neatly folded dress I had set on the nearby table. "You sure ain't packing the right equipment for that kind of work…" Turning his attention back to me, he shifted his weight onto his left foot. "So what *do* you do for a living?"

"I live to fulfill his wishes." The words stuck to the roof of my mouth, were poison on my tongue. Even though I loved Seid still, my loathing was just as great now as it had been then.

"Shit, are you in some kind of trouble?" Cain insisted. "Did you run out on your…your boss, or…" He glared at the hardwood floor, as though blaming it for his poor articulation. His arms fell to his sides, fists clenched. Yet when he opened his mouth to speak, the words faded, and his hard mask shifted.

A surprising fierceness and determination passed along our connection as he lifted his head. "You can stay here as long as you need to."

I cocked my head to the side. "Why?"

Cain shrugged his shoulders and lifted a hand to point to

the scar on his face. "Because I know what it's like to go through tough shit with no one to watch your back. And nobody deserves to be alone."

I had never needed a place to stay before, never needed shelter from the cold or slept through a night, for that matter. All of these things were new to me. And this small kindness from a troubled man who I had already failed, who wore *his* face, pierced my defenses.

Cain's smile fell when I unraveled my legs over the edge of the bed and stood. His chest stilled as I came to him. Keeping my eyes locked to his, I took his fist in my hands and, spreading his long fingers open, pressed his palm over my racing heart. With my free hand, I reached up to cover his. My clan only used this gesture in the most intimate of settings, between family members and—lovers.

His touch burned through the sweater against my skin. I saw my reflection in his dark pupils, how the curse lit my eyes with shades of the dawn. For one infinitesimal moment, our hearts raced in time and then slowed as one.

Pain flashed through his face and made him wince as he tore his gaze from mine, pulling his touch away. Mumbling some excuse under his breath, Cain fled to his room and closed the door behind him.

I sank back onto the magical bed and listened to the sound of the water pounding over his bare skin.

❀❀❀

Tweaking the layer of curtain aside, I watched the storm blanket the outside world in a snow so fine it floated like flour. Here I could almost feel the cold again, rattling against the glass and crawling across it in lacy patterns of ice.

Cain had yet to emerge from his room. As I waited and watched the storm ensue, I was evermore convinced of the solidity of my curse. What better punishment could *he* have given me, really? To be forced to remain inside this enclosed space with a man who wore his face? Cain could never know what torture this was for me.

He should never have seen you in the first place.

Taking my lower lip between my teeth to bite back the sudden chill, I wrapped my arms about my chest. It was still too cold. *I* was cold and determined to find the cure for my current weakness. If Cain did not look the mirror image of Seid then I wouldn't be so distracted, off balance. Far easier to forget humanity. Without the troubling emotions and sensations, this job would be far simpler. If only I could be rid of Cain and the reminders of my past he wore as a mask.

Behind me the radio crackled into life, and I listened to its low electric hum. Without turning, I knew he was there, turning the old knobs and adjusting the volume. Buzzing gave way to a monotone voice on the radio, spouting off facts about the weather that I could have already told Cain about.

Touching my chin to my shoulder, I watched him lean forward in concentration. Water matted his black hair and peppered his cinnamon-brown skin with a fresh sheen. If I shut my eyes, I could still see the god who had bound me, Seid's smile bright as the white sun as he emerged from our latest dip in the sea. I fought the sudden urge to bury my face in his chest and run my fingers through that hair.

He is not Seid.

As if he could sense the shift in my mood, Cain's muscles stiffened, and he lifted his head to observe me in turn. For a moment, I thought I saw a smile touch his lips, and my heart fell with his frown.

"Are you still cold?" he asked. Without waiting for my answer, he sighed. "Who am I kidding? You're thin as a toothpick. Of course you're cold. Hang on a sec." Reaching into a box stuffed in the corner, he sifted through a pile of blankets.

"Have you lived here for very long?" I asked as I wandered about the room. No pictures or paintings adorned the walls, and so little furniture decorated his home, I doubted it.

"A few years," Cain dryly replied. He leaned forward, cradling what looked to be a handmade woolen shawl in his hands. He glanced up, fixing me with a troubled eye before wrapping it over my shoulders.

In my human life, I had never needed warmth, save on the rare cool nights by the sea. Almost immediately, I could feel the wooly warmth cling to my skin and smiled, ready to thank him. But he had already stood and moved to stand by the window. So I marveled, to myself as much as Cain, "It is so warm."

"Well, my mama would be glad someone's using it."

"Why does your mother not live with you?" I always wondered why humans did not live together any longer than necessary. Our home had lodged not only my father's but my mother's parents, until their deaths. Silence was something I only found away from the village, by the sea.

Cain twisted his lean torso to face me and shook his head.

The creases in his brow smoothed as a slow grin began to tug at his cheek. "You just might be the strangest woman I've ever met."

"You think I am mad?" I didn't see the humor in my question, but then again, I was not accustomed to modern humor.

Cain's answering laugh did not feel at my expense. It sounded rough, out of casual use, yet surprisingly pleasant to my ears.

"Nah, if you're mad, I'm definitely certified," he mused. "It's just that most women think less of a man who still lives with his mother. And I'm kind of ashamed to admit this, but it feels weird, talking about my family, when I don't even know your name."

"Orona," I offered, and my lips curled up into an involuntary smile. The warmth I felt trapped underneath his mother's artistry thawed my cold heart. I might have had the strength to fight it if his eyes weren't a blending of colors from the emerald sea. Or if, when he smiled fully at me for the first time, it wasn't like coming home.

"Orona…" Cain inclined his head to me. "What would you like to do today?"

I turned to survey his home and stared at the bed that had been a couch. I pointed with my arm, palm open and extended. "How do you work the magic for that?"

Cain lifted his chin and shoved his thumbs into his sweats pockets. He bit down on his lips after a moment and rocked back on his heels. "Oh, that's way too hard for a beginner. Afraid I'll have to do the honors."

"No, please!" I caught his arm with my hand before he could reach for the end of the extendable bed. He froze, gaze fixed on my touch, smile fading. I pushed aside the strange fluttering in my abdomen to add, "I want to learn." I removed my hand from his arm and clenched my fingers in a vain hope to stop the tingling.

After shaking out of his momentary trance, he offered me instructions. My strength surprised him. We laughed when I leapt forward in my excitement and nearly fell onto the inner wire frame. His arm snaked out to catch me about my waist. He tilted me back against his chest, and I hung limp in his arms from embarrassment.

With the intoxicating scent of his natural underlying scent hovering over me, I braced my hands on his bare arm and slowly straightened into his embrace. A wise immortal would have pulled away from his touch and made him forget ever seeing her. She would go to Lissa and do all in her power to bring the two star-crossed lovers together. She would learn their stories and hopefully help them make a happy ending.

"Come on," he said huskily against my ear, interrupting my thoughts.

I savored the feeling of being held and was determined never to forget it. Did I imagine the way his breath shuddered against my hair?

"Not everybody gets it right the first try," he added in a mock serious tone, but the vibrations in his chest betrayed him.

Whirling around in his embrace, I pumped his chest with my fist and narrowed my eyes. "You are making fun!"

"Me?" He shook his head in denial and almost managed to hide the spark in his eyes before catching my bare fist in his hand. "Oh, I'm always serious about magic."

The human voice trapped in the stereo had finished his long-winded report. Only then did I notice the slow music that had replaced him. The breathy vocals and soft horns reminded me of the club where Cain had first seen me. And it struck me as odd that this young human should favor something of an era gone by.

Threading my fingers through his, I swayed until he followed my time. Long ago, my people danced to the beat of drums and dulcimer, about poles and great pits filled with fire, by the sea that provided for us. I loved to dance. And once I heard the drums beat behind the music, I could remember those same steps again.

Cain watched me with amusement at first as I stepped away from his embrace, pressing our flat, connected palms into the air. My heart thudded in time with the pulse beating in his neck. I coupled our hands slowly and then spun quickly in a circle that lifted my long hair and left me breathless. His mother's shawl fell from my shoulders like a cloak. I released my hold on his hands to lift its fringed edges with my hands and tilted my hips. If I shut my eyes, I could almost hear that ancient drum. I could nearly see my father's and sisters' smiles in the fading firelight.

Cain's voice brought me back. "Orona?" he whispered. His hands were clenched at my waist to hold me in place. After taking in a shaky breath, he said, "I have no clue where you learned to dance like that. And any other time, I wouldn't have stopped you. But for my sanity, could you please not do it in my mother's shawl?" He smirked and alleviated the heaviness that turned his bright blue eyes a rich shade of indigo.

"Of course." I tilted my chin up to better meet him then

gasped to find his lips in my line of sight. The temptation rendered my voice feeble and frail. "It was the harvest dance in my homeland." I was relieved he bowed his head and stole my temptation away.

"The new tides brought in a better catch," I continued, blinking rapidly. "After the meal, we danced until the sun stole back the sky from the moon." Rather than appeasing, I saw how my words upset him. His face looked pained, and I could not bear it. "I am sorry," I said. "Have I upset you?"

He shook his head. "No. It's just the way you talk about the sea… you sound so much like my folks. They loved living on the coast."

I watched as the shadow of his darker memories took shape, hints of the sea and the distant cry of seagulls. Flashes of shadow-drenched faces flickered past my inner eye sporadically, through our connection. I could see a dark-skinned man and a woman with waist-length, straight black hair. And I saw a hairless child with bright and shining amber eyes. I wondered what their names had been, and how long he'd been alone. But not wishing to cause him more pain, I let the questions rest.

"You must teach me more magic," I offered, hoping to distract him from the tension between us. With his answering smile, I knew we had come to some sort of truce.

"You ever play cards?"

"I don't know if purely romantic love can last through anything (it is so based on feelings and attraction, both of which are pretty fickle at times), but I think friendship can, and when the romantic love and friendship get blurred together into one, it makes 'relationship cement,' I think."
— KATE

5

POKER FACE

The cards reminded me of an older game we played with stones when I was a child. Cain enjoyed besting me and commented how they had done this for hours in the barracks. I remembered I was once very competitive and, the moment I mastered his rules, proudly showed it.

For a while, at least, he was content to answer my endless sea of questions. In between breaks while Cain resupplied snacks and drinks, and over the passing of the moon and sun, I learned to love the smooth monotony of our game.

"What do you do at the club?" I asked, gathering a new hand. "You were standing as some kind of guard the night you saw me. Is it your job?"

"Yeah, it helps pay the bills. My day job is actually at this construction site in the city, but I bounce on weekends and most weeknights for my uncle. It's his place, but my cousin keeps things running now. Course, things are a lot different there than they were when I was a kid."

"Where are your parents?" I asked, remembering the brief flash of images Cain had unwittingly shared with me.

He stiffened and laid his card down more roughly than necessary. "Gone. Their ship capsized in a storm when I was still a kid. They were stupid to go out on the water drunk."

I froze at his mention of the ocean, recalling the cry of seagulls through our connection. Of *course* he once lived by the sea. I had smelled it on him the moment we met.

"Rest of my family saw it coming, I guess." Cain threw his cards down with a bitter laugh. "Everyone except my old man. The only thing he listened to was what his bottle of Jack told him to do." Pain drew his brow together and gathered over us in an opaque ominous cloud.

I longed to abandon the game, to fight the darkness and draw light from beyond the storm. My gift hovered just beneath the surface of my skin, ready at a moment's notice.

Save it! Why should you care for the feelings of a human? He is no different than the rest of them.

Cain spread his hands and repaired his broken mask with a tight grin. "Alright, babe, let's see what you've got."

How odd, I mused. Slivers of pain still coursed through the luminous threads connecting us. With every pulse, a tiny grain of light traveled along that link sind reminded me Cain had not forgotten our earlier conversation or his pain. He had simply tucked them aside. Too many humans bottled up their sorrows.

Cain braced his head with his hands when I lay down my cards. He groaned. "Ah, no way!"

"Pay up." I borrowed his phrase and held out my hand.

Cain rolled his eyes and placed another bottle cap in my palm. I fought the pleasant sensation traveling up my arm as our fingers brushed and watched Cain gather our cards to shuffle the deck again.

Between glances, Cain casually mentioned, "So what's your story? You obviously didn't grow up in the States."

He spoke like one who knew. Again I wanted him to forget his curiosity. I wanted to pry apart his layers, uncover *his* secrets. It helped me to separate Cain from Seid. Their mannerisms, while eerily similar, had not convinced me yet this wasn't some cruel joke. There were moments when I half expected Cain's expression to twist into that passionate severity I recalled so vividly. Occasionally I thought I saw him there, hiding in the eyes of a man who had borrowed his face. And I prayed Cain would not strip off his human guise and turn cruel. I reminded myself how much I hated Seid in the first place, how I hated even more my punishment for my supposed wrongs.

I answered his question finally, bitterly, with the past on my mind. "Everyone I knew has been dead an age gone by. But," I paused to catch his reaction, "I too, grew up by the sea. My father owned many boats, but he was always hungry for more. He tried to sell me to a wealthier man. But the match was not… *desirable*…to me." I shuddered to think of the way my husband's fists pummeled my chest. "I was chosen from my sisters for my beauty, he told me."

Seid did not appear as I half expected, tossing aside the human guise to reveal the thunder and lightning trapped inside his skin. Instead, this man named Cain nodded, and the shadows in his face deepened as he said, "He beat you."

My breath caught in my chest. My fingers reached up to clasp the skin covering my rapidly beating heart.

How could he know?

Yet before I could speak, or even think of something to say, he spoke for me.

"I've seen it too many times," he said while bending the deck into unnatural positions. "That's why you came here, isn't it?" he added, drawing my gaze. "To get away from that creep?"

I kept silent, relieved to let him fill in the blanks of my past with whatever was acceptable to his human mind. His eyes were too discerning for me to divulge more.

"I'm not turning you in, if that's what you're worried about," he said as his brows drew lower.

"I would rather hear more of your story," I interrupted his train of thought. There was no doubt in my mind, if he wanted to, Cain could discover all of my secrets. I was forbidden to lie. All he needed to do was ask me the right questions.

Abandoning the cards, Cain leaned against the back of the magical couch and studied me with a wry grin. I froze beneath the weight of that searching gaze. I *knew* that look, for I had seen it countless times on Seid's face. My first love was ever trying to pry apart my human secrets. He always got his way, and I worked my face into a blank look of placid nothingness.

Abruptly the music ceased on the stereo, and the man began his latest report. Cain dropped his scrutiny to favor the cherrywood box with fresh concern.

"Keep cool, ladies and gents. The big freeze may be on us, but we've got more blues on the way. Temperatures continue to drop to record lows, but the storm may not last more than another day..."

Cain's eyes flickered to mine, and I knew I was not imagining his relief. Why he would want to prolong this torture, or face an endless array of questions, was beyond my understanding.

"So." He leaned forward to rest his elbows on his knees. "I think we've had enough poker for one day. Want some dinner? It's got to be pushing eight o'clock by now."

"I do not eat," I reminded him. Even if I was starting to regain my human senses, I had no desire to taste whatever impure concoction he had planned.

"Come on," he said and came to stand in front of me. "Not even supermodels eat *that* little. I may not be the best cook in the world, but my aunt taught me the basics."

I stared at his extended palm doubtfully.

"You said you wanted to learn magic, right?" he added.

I did not hesitate to slip my hand in his warm grasp.

After observing humans for two thousand years, I could tell when the joy had been drained from their lives. Cain's source of joy, whatever that had been, was a secret locked away deeply inside of him. I only knew it had not come from his parents, the nameless faces I shared the memory of through our connection. My first impression of Cain, even when I yet waited for Seid to toss aside the human glamour, was how miserable he was.

Yet for miraculous reasons I did not comprehend, I made him smile—a lot.

"I haven't cooked from scratch in forever," he announced some time later. His lips quirked up into another of his brilliant smiles. "You're lucky I had the right ingredients. Not every day I get the chance to cook for a beautiful woman."

I kept my thoughts to myself as I stirred the odd fluff and chicken together, just the way he had instructed.

Cain chopped fresh—so *he* said—vegetables up and dropped them into the salad bowl. He paused in his work to lean over me with a faux critical eye and tried to hold back his smile. "How you doing over there?"

I held up the spoon with distaste. "Is this...good?"

"Hell, yeah!" he exclaimed. "But you should probably give the poor dumplings a rest. Here." Cain hesitated, a brief glance to check my reaction, before covering my fingers with his and setting the spoon aside. "Let's set the lid so just a little air can come out."

Cain shifted to stand behind me. His chin brushed my shoulder as he leaned over and guided my hand in the proper movements.

I tensed and focused to keep my eyes from fluttering shut at the contact. It was too much. Too much heat and not nearly enough. I could not help being unnerved by him. The metal lid rattled a bit because of my unsteady grip.

A glance over my shoulder revealed his eyes fixed not on the lid, but my face. I opened my mouth to... what? Protest? Ask him to step away? Yet I couldn't, not when the same desire I felt for his touch was reflected in his blue eyes.

"Orona," he whispered then swallowed. The songs switched on the stereo again, and Cain perked up. "Do you want me to show you how *we* dance?"

I fought the urge to grip that metal handle even more

tightly, to run and snatch my cloak and rush to Lissa's aid as quickly as possible. I knew this was dangerous territory. I'd known the moment I found an old god's face reborn in this alluring man. And I was still unconvinced this man was not Seid in human disguise.

So I smiled in answer and allowed Cain to pull me away to the open living space.

We stood as we had before, his hand on my waist and our fingers clasped together, up and away from our bodies. I clutched the square muscle of his shoulder and followed as he stepped back, then led me to sway slowly from side to side.

A flurry of sweet thrills broke past my defenses, lacing up and down my spine as we danced. It was like floating on water once I caught the rhythm in the steps, as I learned to follow his silent cues. The words were out of my mouth before I could rein them in. "How did you learn this dance?"

His warm brown skin flushed that unfortunately familiar shade of rust. Cain skipped a step and nearly stumbled as he formulated his answer. "It's really embarrassing, actually. I had a crush on this girl in high school. She used to come to my uncle's club with her folks on weekends and she knew how to *dance*. So…" He shrugged and looked over my shoulder, anywhere he did not have to see my reaction.

My skin boiled at the thought of another girl in his arms. "You learned for her?"

Stop it! He does not belong to you!

"My aunt taught me," he confessed. "When my cousin caught me practicing with a door and laughed, I punched him in the face. But in the end, *I* got the girl."

Flashes and images of a brown-eyed girl with honey-toned skin danced through our connection. I could feel Cain's pride the moment she let him hold her. It left me with a bitter aftertaste I had no right to have.

His steps slowed when he noticed the tension in my steps, yet he kept his smile firmly in place. "Obviously, it's been a few years since I had any practice. Thanks for not laughing in my face."

I forced a smile but was unable to block the memory of that girl, or of the way Cain still cared for Lissa.

His blue eyes narrowed intently on me. He bowed his head so our noses nearly brushed.

I bit my lip, wondering how I was going to explain the whole supernatural grace thing.

"You're awfully good at this," he said with raised eyebrows. "You pull my leg earlier or something? Here I was thinking you only knew that one sexy dance." He winked, and it was my turn to blush.

At the same moment, his hand slid higher up my waist, and prickles of pleasure darted to my lower abdomen. Fresh air was suddenly in short supply, and I knew I was dancing dangerously near the point of no return. Tripping over my feet on purpose, I feigned a fall in order to push him away.

"Gotcha!" Cain laughed as our foreheads knocked together.

Instead of escaping the human's grasp, I found myself in an even more compromising position, with my breasts pressed to his hard chest. Suddenly everything was entirely too much and too real. It was the way his lips parted to take in badly needed oxygen, how perfectly our hips fit into place, despite the difference in our heights. It was how the thrilling feel of another human's skin made mine come alive.

His heated gaze clouded just like Seid's had before he'd been about to kiss me. What terrified me most wasn't Cain's resemblance to my former love, but the fact I was going to *let* him kiss me. Two thousand years spent hating the one who had cursed me, and I was about to give in, just like he had wanted all along.

My mind was pulled under by the unwelcome memory.

"I will never love you again. You are poison to me!" I shoved him back to no avail.

Seid trapped me in his arms again, eyes flashing the brightest of blues as he laughed. "Oh Orona, you knew what I was from the moment I first stole your lips!"

"You're nothing but a monster!" I cried, despairing, because I knew deep down Seid was right, and chose to forever hate him for it.

Cain's warm breath on my cheek pulled me back to the present. Our lips brushed in the most gentle of caresses. My name escaped the tip of his tongue with a gentle moan. "Orona."

Tears welled in my eyes as I remembered myself and pushed him away.

"Please, no," I begged in a voice that was much too hoarse.

Cain released me instantly, and I stumbled back to cover my face with my hands in shame. Without turning round to face him, I pressed my fingers to my wet eyes and stared at my fingertips. Time froze for the first time in an age as I remembered what this wetness was.

Tears?

I wanted to sob, to laugh or do anything to make my confusion fade. My heart ached for Cain's touch, the embrace of a man I barely knew. But he wasn't just any man, and it wasn't just because he looked just like *him*. It was because this human had somehow reached inside of me, seen through my disguise and made me feel again. And as I hid my gaze behind a golden wall of hair, I wondered if my tears were truly for Cain or the god that shared his face.

"It kind of snuck up on me, I think...he just always wanted to listen and be there, never wanted to pressure me to do anything that I wasn't comfortable with, treated me how I deserved instead of how I had always been treated before..."
—ALLISON

6

WOVEN TOGETHER

Cain was different after I scorned him, almost wary. I watched him eat the food we prepared together and desperately wished I could join him. I ignored the leftovers he packaged in a carton with my name scratched in permanent ink on the lid. He turned off the stereo afterwards and did not turn it on again.

I was grateful because the music made me desperately want his dance.

Without cards or music, we sat silently together on his couch by lamplight and watched the snow fall. As he didn't venture to say anything, I chose to wait. Instead, I used my curse to see past the glass and storm and to the stars beyond. Too many nights I had spent memorizing their patterns, finding their permanence to be my only comfort, the one constant of my long existence.

Cain broke the thick silence so softly I might not have

heard if I were merely human. "You need to eat sometime."

"Do not worry. I have no need for food," I replied too eagerly and released a bated breath after.

Without looking, I could still hear the frustration in his voice as he mumbled, "Starving yourself isn't going to solve anything."

Anger rose in me, the one constant emotion I had lived with the better part of an age. "I am not! If you had ears to listen, you would understand." I watched him pop his knuckles one by one and tried to ignore my inner flinch.

Cain took his time in answering. "I've seen a lot of horrible things and done even more things in my life I'm not proud of. It's not like I'm the right person to judge you, but I know you're hiding something, Orona."

"I can hide nothing from you, Cain," I said truthfully, though I was unable to hold the bitterness from my voice. I was forbidden to lie, and now that I was having my first real conversation in decades, I desperately wanted to.

His gaze found mine in the darkness and seemed to glow like the sun-lit sea.

"Then why do you flinch every time I touch you?" he demanded. "Is it because of *him*?"

"W-who?" I froze and clutched his tee shirt at my neck. Even with his mother's shawl around my shoulders, I felt naked and exposed.

"That's what I figured…that son of a bitch." Cain nodded to himself. "So, which is it? Your man a drug dealer, or worse?"

I shuddered and confessed as little as I was capable. "My father arranged the marriage."

Cain leaned forward, elbow to knee, fingers dragging through curls too short to thread in harsh strokes. His frustration boiled over finally, bruising in its intensity. "Shit! I can't believe your dad would sell you to an asshole stupid enough to *hit* you," he growled.

My heart quelled from how near the truth he came. For the first time since I could remember, I sank against the cushions, exhausted. "It was long ago," I admitted. "And it is not something I want to think about every day."

"I know it's not my place to care. I mean, I barely know you," he began, palm outstretched to me in a silent plea. "I don't understand it. All I know is I feel like I know you, Rona."

My heart leapt at the age-long forgotten nickname. Seid was the only other person to call me that.

"I know it sounds crazy," Cain added, "and I swear I'm not saying this to try and pull the 'we might die in this storm' card." We both grinned as I caught the gist of his joke, and some of the tension eased between us.

Cain eased back onto the couch to better face me, and this time, his smile was haunted. "Sorry I lost my temper. I know that's the last thing you need. I've just been through hell most of my life, and the thought of someone taking advantage of you..." He shook his head, unable to articulate.

So I sighed and gave him what he needed. "I know."

Seid had hated the man who beat me too.

Cain's hand engulfed mine and settled in the space between us. His warmth was only belied by the fervor of his budding affection pulsing along our connection. Before my inhuman eyes, his aura shone around him in shades of gold and stretched with finger-like tendrils toward me. Transfixed, I watched the colors and light trapped within me reach desperately for him in return.

Only hours before, I suffered my first taste of the consequences of breaking Seid's rules. I was already weakened, losing my perfectly honed control. Yet none of this compared to how woefully unprepared I was the moment Cain's aura brushed mine for the first time.

I screamed when the curse immediately retaliated.

My body was thrown off the couch by an invisible force and shoved quickly against the hardwood floor.

"Rona!" Cain shouted, and with reflexes better naturally attuned than mine, he caught me before the impact was too severe.

A troubled silence followed, and I frowned at the black splotches clouding my vision.

"Oh God!" Cain's hands brushed over my trembling limbs, and he turned me over as gently as he could.

I longed to open my eyes but found this impossible as the past flashed behind my closed lids.

"What are you doing here?" I asked the beautiful stranger. Because this was my escape, my secret retreat, and I was unhappy to find another man in my way. Had I not suffered enough from their kind?

His smile was dazzling, revealing almost perfect white teeth. The sun was blinding behind him as he laughed and answered, "Waiting for you, Rona."

The moment my gaze locked with his, something within me pulled rapidly toward him, a twisting, living twine quickly braiding together.

On second glance, I noticed how his brown skin glowed like the setting sun as his black curls flew wildly in the wind of a coming storm.

I wanted him like I'd never wanted anything in my life.

I rushed to our place, our secret cave, where nothing and no one could ever find us. Here, I would always be safe because it was in his domain. And I desperately needed to feel safe now. The rain masked my tears, but it couldn't wash away the fear growing in my heart.

Waves crashed against the nearby rocks, a violent tempest. Cries of panic echoed from the docks and alerted me to the effect my mood was having on Seid. It had frightened me at first, how the winds and the seas reflected his moods. When we kissed, the skies had never appeared more heavenly, nor the seas a more brilliant shade of sapphire blue.

Now in his fear and fury, the seas churned and tossed about, rocking against the shoreline with increasingly higher gusts of water.

Seid was already waiting with his arms open for me. In his fierce embrace, I forgot my madness and the tears spilling down our cheeks afresh.

When he cried, the rains escaped the dark clouds above.

"I'll kill them all, Rona," he promised with a rumble of thunder. "I wish you would let me destroy them for what he's done to you."

I pressed a hand to his chest. "Please don't hurt them. They don't mean to be cruel. He is to be my family now, Seid!"

"No!" Thunder and lightning struck in a cataclysmic boom that *shook the rocks at our feet. Seid braced my face with his hands and breathed into me, "I am your family, Rona."*

A hoarse voice nearly screamed my name in the distance, calling me back to the present until I came fully back to myself.

"Rona?" Cain's voice hitched as he spoke over me. "Oh God, let her stay with me. I swear I won't go back to it...*never* again if you'll just..." He murmured more prayers in my ear, rocked with me on his chest. Wetness covered my cheeks, just like in my memories.

"I'm so sorry, baby." The hands that caressed my back trembled, and he choked on his own words. "I shouldn't have pushed you so hard when I don't know what you came from. I always push too hard. But you're so different from anyone I've ever met—I thought maybe I'd finally found someone who could understand. Christ," he murmured bitterly to himself, "she's gonna think you're crazier than you already are. Why didn't I get my prescription renewed?"

Moaning, because the words stuck too tightly to my mouth, I managed a weak reply. "I thought *I* was the mad one."

Cain froze above me, and then a bright bubble of happiness filled the space between us. Cain laughed as he brushed my damp hair off my forehead. "No, baby, that would be me. You can thank PTSD for that."

I had no idea what PTSD stood for, yet for some foolish reason, my soul ached to comfort his. Had I not just endured the curse's warning for breaking the rules? I ignored the aftereffects of the attack on my body to press an unsteady palm to his heart.

"You did not do anything wrong, Cain. This was my fault.

I forgot myself. If I had stayed away when we met, then none of this would have happened."

And you would have never known what it was like to feel again.

Cain's jaw clenched, and he replied, almost as if he had heard my thoughts, "Life's too short to dwell on regrets, Rona. Trust me."

My nerves were still electrified, overshot with a lightning force. I knew exactly how it felt to be pierced by the bone-melting power of a lightning bolt, after all. But Seid's unspoken message was clear to me now. I had allowed myself to become too close to this human. I shifted at the realization, desperate to be out of Cain's arms and far, far away from this place.

The warmth and relief I had seen shining so fully in his eyes before faded, and he stood. "Is there anything I can get you?"

"No, I am well." My voice trembled, betraying me. I looked at anything and everything else but the way Cain's brow furrowed and pain darkened his golden aura. I wanted to push the hair aside and smooth that brow with a kiss, anything to keep the look of dejection from his face.

"I know I acted like an ass earlier. I shouldn't have tried to kiss you, but it just felt—right."

I pretended I didn't see the flare and flash of determination steeling his blue gaze.

"I swear I won't try to touch you again, not unless you—"

Unless I want him to, I thought. And if we weren't in danger of creating a bond of our own, a wild, terribly beautiful one, I would have kissed more than his brow then.

"*I love and am loved in return, but for me,
l'amore is nothing more than a literary device.*"
—TAMMY

7

FINDING LISSA

Now I knew for certain I wasn't only risking my existence by staying here. By letting him close to me, I was risking Cain's life.

I stole out from between the covers of the magical couch while he slept. I shook out my folded cloak and slipped it over my shoulders, then pulled the cowl over my head. My gaze shifted from the window to the wall before I could stop myself. My immortal eyes could easily see through the thin wall separating me from Cain's sprawled-out form. He slept so peacefully, his tattooed arms thrown over his head and his fingers clenching the pillowcase.

After sucking in a ragged breath, I squeezed my eyes shut. I didn't want to feel again. Being numb to love and desire had once been a part of my curse. Now, it was the only reason I continued to follow the call wherever it would take me. Feelings might have been my downfall, but I had forgotten how delicious they could be.

Days ago, as I left my latest assignment safe in their beach home, images of their future flashed rapidly in my head, and I ached for things I could never have. Until I found Cain and Lissa. Their emotions were tied to me, to help me aid or test them as I saw fit. It was addictive, feeding off human emotions. Now I wondered if the general apathy I'd existed within was a gift compared to the way Cain left me transfixed on a compulsion for more.

Was this how I made Seid feel? My innards twisted at the thought. One thing I knew for certain. If I didn't leave tonight, I would damn us all to whatever punishment Seid determined.

So I willed the curse to encompass me and relinquished the things that made me feel human. Lissa and Cain's connection had diminished into a faint golden thread now, ready to break and snap at the slightest pull. I cringed as I lifted a finger to test its strength. The last time I was sent to salvage such a connection as this, it snapped the first evening I observed the couple together. Yet I had felt the pull and draw of Cain and Lissa so strongly, I practically flew across the country. How could it have reduced so quickly to this?

I wanted to rail at Seid then, to beat his chest with my fists for wasting my time. Anger was an emotion I was much more acquainted with, so I soaked it up like a sponge, snatched hold of the thread connecting Cain with Lissa, and let it carry me.

The floor buckled beneath my feet and then simply disappeared. Homes and the people safely inside them blurred past me, then the homeless having vacated the streets for their shelters. While the city slept beneath a layer of ice, I let the hum of their emotions fill me until it choked me.

Soon I wouldn't feel so human anymore and could forget this weakness.

Despite the cruel winterscape, a few lone stragglers haunted the alleyways, shooting up, chugging alcohol, and walking off the buzz that made them immune to the cold.

Isn't that what you're doing? Drowning in their emotions so you can forget?

City lights blurred behind the tears filling my eyes, and I wiped them furiously away. Once I was like them, naïve enough to believe in third, fifth and seventh chances. I flirted with death like an old lover.

Had I known the true face hidden behind Seid's charm, I would have listened to my sisters' warnings. Though they never saw him, they did see me after the hours I'd spent lost mapping the contours of his body. Every time I returned from our hideaway beneath the sea, I lost pieces of myself.

I had been beaten by my husband, the man my father bound me to. My time with Seid was meant to be brief, one last dalliance before duty. But with every passing moon, my hatred for my father's choice grew. My sisters noticed first. I should have kept my thoughts to myself. Maybe then my sisters wouldn't have betrayed my secrets to the servants. Maybe then Seid would have stayed his fury.

Lissa was on the other side of the city, lost in the sleekest of neighborhoods I saw replicated in every city. Every metropolis needed a center where power players could stake their claim.

As I flew above the hard ground, I remembered the limo Lissa and Derek escaped in, and I wasn't surprised the thread had led me here. What did surprise me was the emptiness of many of these homes. Here were the grand palaces of modern-day royalty. And it would seem riches did not guarantee happiness any more than it had in my time.

Lissa's flame of the moment had brought her to his personal palace at the very top of an exclusive suite. After passing through the outer walls, I breathed in the scent of wealth and glanced up through the ceiling. It was so different from Cain's apartment, far more richly furnished but somehow colder.

Stop thinking about what does not belong to you!

I returned my focus to the fragile cord and lifted my hand toward it. Weak though it may be, the connection between Lissa and Cain was strong enough that I was lifted up. Weightless, I passed through every obstacle so easily I could nearly forget what it had meant to be in Cain's grounding presence.

When I opened my eyes again, I was standing on a solid glossy floor. My body solidified and quickly acclimated to my new surroundings. All light was dimmed or snuffed completely, though I took in the thoughtless perfection of the apartment in one fell swoop. The flat was furnished with the latest in exclusive tastes, with wide curtain-masked windows overlooking skyscrapers. Two dirty plates and a half-finished bottle of wine sans glasses sat atop the bar. Clothes were strewn about the floor of the tiled hallway. Lissa's shawl, coat, and pumps had been carelessly tossed aside with the man's tie and polished black shoes.

Have they left the bed at all? I thought with a twist of my lips.

This storm should have given Lissa ample time to make the ideal conquest. She had been Derek's partner of choice to wait out the deepening freeze with. But the trail I had followed still linked her and Cain together. No matter what she and this stranger shared, a shard of her heart belonged to Cain.

Muffled sounds escaped the bedroom, and I instinctively moved toward the door. Stepping through the solid matter, I pushed easily through the wall and stood amid the shadows of Derek's bedroom. His bed took up a solid corner of space, and there he lay sprawled on his stomach across it in a dreamless sleep. Following the outline of his body clearly revealed the appeal he must have, but there was something lacking from him that I had not felt the other night.

Where is Lissa?

Another muffled sound—a sob?—came from behind the bathroom door. A faint light escaped around the doorframe, and I couldn't shake the foreboding in my heart as I approached.

The instant I stepped foot through the door, I was met by the stench of blood and the jarring sight of my reflection. Hidden from her eyes I may be, I cleaved to the shadows and avoided the light.

Lissa's glorious unbound hair was gathered loosely in a band behind her head. Her honey-brown skin looked too pale and drawn against her gaunt frame. With her hands braced on the sink counter, she lifted her head and stared at her reflection. Her leafy-green eyes were red with tears.

A far cry from the laughing woman from the other night—further still from the smiling girl Cain shared his first dance with.

I wondered briefly if she could see me as Cain had, watching over her shoulder from the darkness like a specter.

How fitting…

Was I not a creature of the darkness now, trapped by my

own selfish desires? Because of my selfishness, something had gone horribly wrong for Lissa. Her aura was broken, torn nearly to shreds.

How to explain an aura to human eyes? It was like the swirling of every feeling or emotion you have or will soon have, color coded. Sometimes it sprung from their skins like a divine halo, while others it hung like a bleak cloud or blurred their features in a thick gray fog. Most often it appeared like the northern lights, a shimmering of color so rich it was impossible to name them all. I have seen every color, naked or invisible to the human eye.

Lissa's aura emanated from her a slick red steam and matched the blood staining her lips and spattered on her upturned palms.

Clenching my teeth against the harsh metallic scent, I focused on her scantily clad form. The lingerie looked uncomfortable, and the constrained cut didn't seem to fit with the vivacious young woman I had glimpsed on the dance floor.

Despair poured from her glassy eyes as she breathed steadily in and out. With shaking hands, she held up the palms full of dripping blood, and a hoarse wail broke past her lips. Twisting the sink knob quickly, she then ran her hands under the stream of water until it steamed and nearly scalded her skin.

"Pull it together, chica," she whispered as she grabbed a soap bar and scrubbed between her fingers. The overhead light illuminated the bruises imprinted down her back, the marks where Derek's too-rough touch had been.

A flash of images darted through my mind of Derek throwing her onto the bed and grasping her until she screamed, not from ecstasy but agony. I could feel Lissa's pleasure quickly turning to fear and then pain. Pressure filled her ears until all sound was blocked out, save for a dull ringing. The air I breathed seemed to stifle and thicken until I was clutching my throat and clinging to the curse to keep me hidden. The images called forth unbidden plunged me into emotions I never wanted to relive again. Yet in the darkness behind my eyelids, I could still see, smell, and feel everything so clearly.

"Wait, please! I promise to obey!" I cowered, scrambling backward, trying to shield my already broken body. The whip in my husband's hands hung limp at his side, stained by my blood. His chest heaved with the aftermath of his rage.

"You certainly shall obey, Orona. I will not stand sharing my possessions with anyone else. Our union is little more than a business deal, but your father and I signed a contract binding you to me. Do you know what it says of my rights in the case of your infidelity?" His dark eyes blackened to pitch as he took another step and loomed over me.

I shivered, nodding. "I understand. I will obey."

I ran to the cliffs as soon as I was able to escape the eyes of his guard, though the scabs from my wounds were barely healed. Every breath I took was agony, and every sob jarred the ragged skin of my back.

"Seid!" I gasped and fell at his feet. Had he not caught me, I would have fallen to the earth. At the simple touch, relief and the full weight of what I had endured settled in.

Today his skin was as dark as the clouds looming over us, his eyes swirling with tempests. "Rona, I felt your pain! Who would dare to touch you like this?" Thunder rumbled in the billowing skies, tail-ending his words.

"It was him," I sobbed. "One of his servants saw us together." I shook, already seeing double. My wounds were opening, and my lover cursed as violently as the lightning that parted the seas.

The sound of Lissa's cries brought me back to the present as she crooned over herself. "It's okay… We're going to be okay, baby girl. We're going to be okay." Lissa buried her face in her hands as she crumpled to the floor. Silent sobs shook her, breaking up her prayers as she rocked against the wall.

Slowly, I turned to meet my reflection and looked into the eyes of the creature I had become. Clashing colors trapped within those familiar pupils were stained by a fresh wave of tears. The creature in the mirror gaped and slowly lifted her fingers to wipe them away. For two thousand years, I had allowed myself to accept Seid's curse, to become soulless. But I still remembered a time when I was vulnerable and human, as weak as this woman unaware of my vigil.

Guilt was a feeling I hadn't allowed myself in ages. Why should I feel guilty when it had been Seid who cursed me for things beyond my control? Over the centuries, I had sought to appease the curse, but my task had long lost its luster. Perhaps this is why so many marriages, relationships, and first loves had failed, in spite of my efforts?

Because I did not want them to. Because I had given up.

I could no longer pretend this was about my unjust punishment. I had not been visited by Seid in a thousand years and was sure he had found another woman to seduce. The love of gods was a fickle thing, in my experience.

Once I had been like this broken woman and lost my chance at happiness. For the first time in two thousand years, I found myself wanting to give Cain and Lissa what I'd never had—a happy ending.

"…understanding each other without words…"
—LISA

8

DANGEROUSLY BEAUTIFUL

My mission had changed overnight, infused with new vigor. I would do anything to renew the link between my couple, but first I needed to know them better. To begin, I needed to find what had linked them together in the first place. While Cain slept through the early morning, I explored his home.

A small closet stood next to the door of his room, facing the kitchen bar. Little in the apartment truly reflected the deeper layers of Cain's personality. To know him, I must dig deeper than I had ever cared to before. Had I been human still, I might have never found the courage to pry into another person's belongings. Then again, I might have anyway. A darker part of me warred against duty, wanted to know exactly why he had picked *her*.

So I turned the knob slowly and pulled the closet door open to peek inside. In the dusty darkness, I breathed in the scents of the salty sea and lingering spices. My father made his living trading in spices and other expensive wares. Once, I had known every one of their scents by heart.

I peered deeper into the musty corners, and my skin brightened in answer to my need. Colors shifted, luminous, until a rainbow blend danced over the walls, altering the pigment of my skin. I reached beneath a sea of clothes until my hands grasped a handle and pulled.

I had forgotten how strong I was. The large, oddly shaped case flew up into me, sending me back several steps. Wincing, I held my breath, and I waited for the inevitable crash and tumble of the pile setting itself to rights. Instead I stood rock-still with the long black case pressed against my chest.

Cain's steady breathing continued uninterrupted on the other side of the wall.

The case was made of two rounding curves and a long neck. I set it on the magical bed, flipped open the clasps, and then pried open the top. The wooden instrument was darkly varnished, studded with metal and strings over a bored-in hole. I lifted the long neck, and I clutched the instrument closer to my chest. The strings were cool and taut beneath my fingers, and I smiled as sound escaped with the vibrations.

"It's out of tune." Cain's voice startled me to find him standing in the open doorway with an inscrutable look on his face.

"You are a musician," I said, happy he wasn't too upset by my intrusion.

Cain reached out and took the instrument from my hands. He held it before him with a pinched, inscrutable look as he lost himself to the sleek track of wood. "My uncle gave me this when I was just a kid. I even remember watching him perform on stage some nights. We lived in the flat above the club. Not a very practical place for raising kids, I know."

Cain glanced up at me and smirked as he began adjusting the knobs at the end of the long neck. "I used to sneak down some nights, when I was supposed to already be in bed, of course, and just listen. One night, he catches me backstage messing with his guitar and says, '*You need to learn blues before you play anything else, boy.*' Then he just hands it to me and, well, you can guess the rest." Cain pressed the flat back of the guitar to his chest and gently plucked the metal strings.

I held my breath in anticipation and was disappointed when the only sounds that escaped the guitar were more vibrations. His fingers stilled, and I asked, "Is it broken?"

Cain caught my eye, and he grinned as he replied, "It's an electric guitar. You can't really hear the music unless it's plugged in."

I leaned forward to stroke the blue-painted wooden surface of the guitar and watched the muscles in his forearms twitch. "Did you learn?"

"Yeah…practiced every day, even thought I was B.B. King for a while." His smile faded, and he set the guitar back in its case. "But that was before my aunt got sick." He shut the case, and as it clicked back into place, so ended his tale.

Setting my hand on the case, I persisted. "You should play again."

A flicker of surprise passed through our connection before he replied in a heavy tone, "I don't know if that's a good idea, Rona."

"I know what it is like to forget your dreams," I said, "to lose yourself in darkness…" My fingers burned when Cain gently removed them from the case. For some reason, it was difficult to speak, and I refused to question why.

He shut his guitar back in its closet without responding. I watched as he averted his gaze and crossed the room to check the pace of the snowstorm beyond the curtain. Every good emotion I had sensed from him seemed to be sucked through that frosted window.

"Did you want a shower?" Cain called over his shoulder. "Thought you might want to go first, before the hot water heater is out for good. Couple more days of this weather, and it won't last much longer in this building." His biceps bulged with each clench of his fists.

"How does it work?"

Shocked out of his reverie enough to face me, Cain stared at me and then laughed. "You're kidding? Rona, you can't tell me you've never had a shower before."

I reached behind my back to twist my waist-length curls—an old human habit—and watched him warily.

Cain shifted into the light, and I could see the carefree man I knew through cards and dinner and dancing. I wanted this man.

Please let this storm end soon.

His eyes followed my movements as I crossed my legs and bit my lip. So far, I had only managed to anger or amuse him and was no closer to learning the story behind him and Lissa.

"Okay, that's it," he finally said as he crossed the room and extended a hand. "You just lost your last chance to say no."

"Do I smell that bad?" I teased and then grinned like an idiot as he led me through his bedroom.

"I'll draw the water for you." Pointing at the various knobs, he instructed, "Twist this way to make it hot and this way for cold." He glanced over his shoulder to see if I understood.

Blood rose to my cheeks when he caught me focused on the exposed muscles of his midriff instead. I crossed the small space to follow his instructions better and pretended not to notice how his gaze raked over me briefly in turn.

"What do I do when I am finished washing?" I felt curiously exposed and in need of his mother's shawl.

"Just push it back in," he quietly replied. "Shout if you need help with anything." He paused to smile once more before shutting the door behind him.

ᴑᴓᴑ

Two days ago, I wouldn't have cared whether I took a shower or not. It wasn't like I could have felt its heat. But, oh, how glorious was the warmth of the clear spray and the steam drifting on air now. Every nerve stood on end beneath my skin and tingled beneath the heat. It recalled memories better left forgotten.

How he managed to steal into the baths was beyond my understanding. But my lover was the sea, forged by the stormy skies above them. So why should he not come to me in the steam of the public baths?

My sisters laughed nearby, but no others had come to this corner of the baths. I had come here for solitude, to avoid their endless questions and their fear of me.

Seid slipped an arm around my waist and ran his

hand over my bare skin with the other. I shivered when he breathed against my ear. "Leave them behind, Rona. Come home with me tonight instead."

"I cannot," I whispered as I fought for control. Yet I was clay beneath his skilled hands, powerless to fight him.

Seid's lips worked against the nape of my neck and traced the curve of my shoulder. "I am weary of waiting, my love." He groaned. "Come now, please." And then his voice changed to hint at his true nature, carrying the crash of thunder in its depths as he growled, "Come."

"Are you coming out of there sometime today, Rona?" Cain chuckled to himself on the other side of the bathroom door. "You've been in there more than thirty minutes, babe. Pretty sure you've already used all the hot water in the building, but I won't tell the neighbors if you don't."

I clutched the faded wall tiles, sucked in several rapid breaths, and struggled to find a better grip with my trembling limbs.

The water had run cold.

For an awful moment, I heard not Cain, but *his* voice commanding me to come to him, to obey. Leaping quickly from beneath the frigid spray, I held onto the shower curtain to keep balance.

"Rona?" Cain's voice was pressed tighter to the door, his hand upon the handle. "You okay?"

"I'm fine!" I gasped when my feet hit the bathroom rug and reality settled back in. I was with Cain. I was safe.

Through the foggy haze, I caught my reflection in his shower mirror. My skin glowed in the fluorescent light. Every patch of skin radiated the bold and brilliant colors of the sunset and the waters they had overtaken the moment of my damnation. My irises carried these colors constantly within them, fading from one to the next depending on my mood. This was one reason why I could never reveal myself to another human. There had always been the risk I couldn't hide my true nature from them.

It was easier to wait until the final moment to unveil myself. Far easier for them to brush aside a fleeting memory of an angel than a living god.

My body began to tremble harder then, and I squeezed my eyes shut as I tried to stamp out the emotions that had triggered the curse. But when I opened my eyes, the angel remained. And I could no longer deny the fact I was losing control.

"You don't sound fine," Cain said with more than a hint of concern. "Are you decent?" He waited for my reply, but his words had already fallen on flat ears. I was gasping because of the chills, and because my innermost fears were manifesting before my eyes.

You will not lose control!

I had left the shower on. How did it turn off again? With my skin so sensitive at the moment, even the floor felt hard and unnatural.

Water had escaped past the curtain and made the way slick, but I saw too late. My feet slid, and I braced my hands out to catch my fall as I slipped. Had I not been so lost to the sensation of falling, I might have caught myself rather than crash back into the spray with a heavy thud.

"Rona!" Cain crashed through the door.

I cried out in surprise at the pain in my backside and in my wrists. I stared at them and watched the curse begin to instantly heal the cuts and fill me with numbness once again.

Somehow Cain managed to turn off the shower and lift me into his arms in the blink of an eye. My throat welled up as our connection flashed back into being with the weight of his emotions. They surrounded me, coupled with my own fear of being *seen*.

Cain made no comment about the glow of my eyes, or how the colors trapped in my skin began to leak out onto him. His face was clouded by dissipating steam, though his dark-blue eyes burned brightly into mine. I scarcely registered the subtle shift of his steps, the brush of the towel he had grabbed and wrapped like a shield around my body.

After setting me on his bed, Cain flipped on the bedside lamp and lifted my hands to inspect them.

They've already healed.

"Are you hurt?"

I shook my head and sighed when he climbed onto the bed and wrapped me in his arms again.

"Rona," he began as he grasped my back and clutched me closer to him.

On impulse, I wrapped my arms around him, no matter that my towel was slipping, or that he did not belong to me. I relished being so close, so warm again. Had I spent two thousand years cold?

"You know, you're making it really hard for me not to touch you right now."

"I'm sorry," I said as I pulled away.

"Don't be," he was quick to answer. With surprising gentleness, he pulled my towel back in place and then left to clean up the mess I had made.

⌀⌀⌀

Energy was running low in this part of the city. Ice raced to snap power lines and freeze up pipes. While the people did what they could, only I knew the storm was about to cease and the weak sun would reclaim their world. I *might* have used my gift a bit to help it along.

Clearly it was no longer safe for me to remain trapped with Cain. The curse wouldn't be satisfied until I learned more of the connection between him and Lissa. How could I test their love if I didn't understand them? Otherwise I would have never been brought here. I was inexorably drawn to true love, and now I had broken the most important of all rules by getting involved.

Every time I thought of Lissa, I saw the blood in her hands and the hopelessness in her green eyes and felt like dying all over again. This is why Cain's gentleness affected me so, why I was the worst of people for savoring it while I could.

Cain did his best to joke and ease the awkward tension between us. His favorite and most annoying method was the endless sea of questions he asked me in the hours following my shower.

"Are you sick, Rona?" he began over breakfast.

"I am cursed." I gave the simple truth.

He pondered this through our first three games of cards. Even as he told me more stories of his childhood by the sea and the nightclub after, I knew he was thinking of it.

At least he is giving you the answers you were looking for, my inner voice taunted.

After breakfast, I learned how much Cain loved working on boats and how much he missed surfing the Atlantic waves. In my mind, I could so clearly picture Cain at one within the crest of a wave.

"You have to imagine the power behind it, Rona. You can't predict it. One minute you could be flying, and the next you're crushed," he said.

I knew far better than he could ever guess. Seid used to use his power to show me the eye of the storms and the tumultuous sea depths in a hurricane.

After lunch, Cain struggled with himself before finally asking the question I'd sensed pressing against his mind. "You know my shaving mirror, the one in the shower?"

I peered up at him and willed numbness to cool my features. Feelings were too dangerous to tamper with now, and he mustn't see my nervousness.

"Well, did you know it's broken? It shattered all over the floor when you fell." Cain ran a hand over his jaw. "The glass was covered in blood. But I didn't see any blood on you, or glass sticking out of your hands."

"Sorry about your mirror," I offered with just a hint of a smile.

Cain paused, incredulous, before saying, "Nobody falls on glass and comes out without a scratch, Rona."

There was more behind his words, a building need for things I should *not* tell him. Yet I was certain he had seen the shifting colors trapped within my skin.

"I heal quickly," I finally said and instantly regretted it.

Cain released a breath and rested his head between his hands. His gaze was as blue as the emerald sea when it slowly rose to meet mine.

I closed my eyes and reluctantly opened myself to his emotions. Wild, untamed anger underlay an overwhelming love in his heart. My breath began to pick up in time with the images of high mountainous waves and tempests, and when I tried to cut the connection, the images pushed back even harder.

This was new and somewhat frightening. I was unused to losing a battle of wills with any human. Instead of breaking the link, I felt another wave of desire and deeper longing, so strange for one so young, so *new*. I shuddered and drank deeply from his hidden feelings, unable to help myself, enjoying what I hadn't in ages. And what unsettled me most was I could not tell whether this love was meant for me or for Lissa.

I opened my eyes abruptly and stood, too afraid to look into his eyes. I was too afraid he would see and know what I had just dared. I moved to the window and brushed aside the curtain to press my palm to the glass. Its coolness helped to numb my thoughts and slow the rapid beat of my heart.

How could you be so stupid? I wanted to scream at myself for giving into the temptation to feed off his feelings. All my careful efforts to squash away my weakness for their sakes had failed within twelve hours.

I stared as heat from my hands thawed the frost lacing the window. My breath billowed in an translucent filmy layer around it.

The sun was rising high above the snow clouds, though not as quickly as I had called for it. I could not control the weather like Seid, but I could manipulate circumstances to protect what must be protected at all costs. If I was going to protect Lissa and Cain's love, the sun *must* come, I reasoned.

Cain adjusted the dial of the stereo, and the voice of some long-dead singer crooned through the antique speakers. Even without turning round, I could feel his eyes on me. A whisper of a thrill laced my spine with each step he took toward me. And then he was simply there, reaching above my head to push the curtain fully aside.

"Tell me about her," I said, breaking the silence, and hoped he would forget his curiosity.

Cain's arm fell lifelessly as he fell back a step. "What are you talking about?"

"Lissa," I answered with a glance over my shoulder. I expected his cheeks to blush russet, or to see some other sign of his discomfort. Instead my heart fell to the pit of my stomach against the harsh glare he regarded me with.

"How did you know about Lissa?"

I fastened my eyes to the window so they wouldn't betray me. "I saw the way you looked at her the other night."

"And you just made up your mind about us after one look? You don't know anything about us, Rona."

"I know that you are alone," I insisted, "and she might have left with another man, but she wished it had been you." My assurances were unfounded, of course, but I had to give him something. I could no longer pretend this was about me.

Cain laughed. "If you believe that, then you *definitely* don't know Lissa. Derek's her flavor of the month. She's always looking for a new wallet to dip her hands in. Always been that way..."

I watched Cain's reflection in the window as he paced behind me with his hands on his head. Several almost expressions crossed his face, from ire to consternation and then disbelief. "Where the hell's this coming from, anyways? Did you honestly think that me and Lissa were still..."

My gasp was too loud. Cain froze just behind me, and I clutched the glass pane tighter to root myself in place.

Do not let him see.

"Rona," Cain groaned. "I would *never* try to kiss you if I was with someone else."

I shuddered as his long fingers clasped my shoulder.

Sometimes the mind crosses fire with the heart, and no matter how strongly it screams, the heart always wins. My mind was screaming at my stupid body to move away, to do something. But when I allowed Cain to turn me around, what I found stole my breath away. His heart shone through his eyes, and not for her but for me.

Tears filled my eyes once again. "What are you saying?" I held my breath, wondering what the curse would do in light of this forbidden bond between us. If I tried to reach for his aura again, to test our bond, would it truly kill me? Would it harm him?

"I don't know what happened in the shower this morning," Cain said. "I've been going over what I saw all day, trying to make sense of it. Every time I feel like I'm close to the answers, I get distracted."

He laughed, and I couldn't help but smile in return. How could he know he was breaking my heart as much as mending it?

His fingers trailed a fiery pattern along my neck and cupped my jaw as he closed the distance between us. "It's like I've been asleep all my life," Cain whispered, "but when I saw you, I woke up." He chuckled low and shook his head, adding, "That sounded a lot less cheesy in my head…but it's true."

I smiled when Cain's forehead pressed onto mine and another wave of his emotions bled into me. My lips parted at the addictive rush of the strongest emotions of any human I had known. I was cursed and forbidden to know love again. It was meant to be impossible.

"Rona, I really want to kiss you now."

My eyes fluttered shut as his lips brushed mine, and I fell into him. So long had I been without love, I was beginning to think his affection would become a crippling drug to me. If I plunged in, I might never claw back out of my addiction.

Of course the curse chose that moment to interrupt, with a sharp jabbing pain to my temple. A groan fell from my mouth as I pressed my hands against his chest and used all my strength to hold him at arm's length. "Wait," I pleaded with him, for both our sakes.

Cain flinched as though I had struck a physical blow.

I pulled away from him until my back was pressed against the window. Grasping my aching head in my hands, I said, "I'm sorry, Cain, but what you feel for me is impossible. I can never have you because you don't *belong* to me. Can't you understand that?"

"Who says? Did Lissa say something to you? Is that why you brought her up earlier?"

"No, she said nothing to me. I only wanted you to remember your love for her." I longed for my heart of stone, anything but this crushing pain echoing through our bond.

Cain shook his head. "Orona, that's just—I don't even want to begin to—why can't you just tell me the damn truth? What are you so afraid of?"

His arms were longer than mine, so of course he barely needed to reach to grasp my shoulders. His heat combined with the cold against my back gave me chills. I blinked past the tears blurring his troubled features. I was breaking the most important rule by giving into him, but had I not broken all the others?

"I am afraid of myself, but most of all you, Cain." A sob escaped as I whispered, "I am afraid you will see *me*."

When his lips crashed into mine, the world as I knew it shattered to pieces.

9

FALLEN

My blood was on fire, a molten lava stream coursing beneath the violent sea, my nerves the charged earth still pulsing with the force of a lightning strike. I let out a desperate sigh of relief.

Cain crushed me to his chest with one arm, while the other sank greedily into my hair and drew me closer. Our lips grasped and our tongues tasted too roughly in a clumsy rush that was somehow perfect, and so wonderful I couldn't stop smiling.

He tasted like the warm summer seas, melted honey, and fresh rain—an impossibly familiar taste. My tears dried against each brush of his lips on my cheeks and my eyelids. I longed to crawl into him and never come out.

Carry me forever, I wanted to tell him, because I was so weary of holding myself up. The golden light Cain carried within filled and expanded between us, weaving through my aura in an unstoppable web. It came as nothing more than a sliver, a tendril trapped in the vast web of tangled emotions. For that one moment, it wasn't his emotions I was feeding off of, but *mine*. With this one sliver of true feeling, I knew I would always crave him, just as I had craved the god who cursed me.

The pain was unbearable as Seid inflicted his wrath on me with the force of his will. Those glorious blue eyes were frozen into cold and dark seas, indifferent to my screams. In all our tumultuous and tender times together, I had never believed he would use his power on me.

"I pledged myself to you!" I cried. "Why are you doing this?"

"You know why," he seethed.

"But I didn't truly betray you! You would have known if I had! Please, it is not their fault, Seid. Spare them, and punish me!"

My pain ceased, and a cruel smile transformed his features into something dangerously beautiful.

"Will you avow yourself to my will?"

"Anything."

I opened my eyes to my own reflection. Within Cain's irises, I saw my power fill me as the curse reawakened. Pain pricked at my skin with the potency of a water dragon's tail. I gasped and began to pull away, but then Cain deepened our kiss. And then I realized I was lying on the couch with Cain poised above me. I had not even felt the shift in our positions, lost to the feel of him and my memories.

Now it was too late to warn him.

I saw in Cain's eyes that he knew what was going to happen before I could pull away. The light grew into an unstoppable

force, burned beneath my skin and flushed out of my palms.

Cain yelled as the curse threw him off of me and into the adjacent wall.

Aftershocks wrecked my nerves then numbed them as I clung to couch cushions in horror. I don't know how long I lay like this, only that at some point, Cain picked me up and carried me to his bed. Memories of my past life flashed behind my closed lids as I slept.

I awoke to lamplight spilling over the fine wrinkles marring Cain's brow. I pressed my fingertips to his lips in wonderment. Even after my curse attacked him, he was still here, holding me.

Surely I had broken the rules for the last time. I had half expected to wake up in another part of the world completely, inhumanly numb and on the way to another pair of failing lovers.

"You're still here," I whispered.

Cain's eyes shifted into a darker indigo as he struggled over his words. "I've been having these crazy dreams the last two nights," he finally replied.

"Dreams?" My voice wavered as I added, "Of what?"

He traced my cheekbones with a calloused finger, following an invisible trail along my jaw, then the curve of my lips. "I dreamed of a storm, like the one that killed my folks."

I gasped and pressed a hand to rest above his heart. "I am sorry."

Cain shook his head with a smile and caught my hand before I could pull away again. "In the dreams, I'm in the sea, or on a beach, and there's always another storm waiting for me. I feel like I'm losing my mind every time, until the moment you come to me. It's the same feeling I get when we're together, like I can finally breathe again."

My breath hitched in my throat at his words. Our legs had threaded together, or rather my leg was trapped between his. Whatever defenses the curse had built up were melted away by his words and his touch. Why did it choose to fight and then give into this connection I shared with Cain the next minute?

"You remember my friend Chloe at the club?" Cain said, "Well she never saw you. She thought I was playing some joke on her, talking to myself. It was like you were invisible to her, and I could have sworn she looked right through you at one point. You looked so surprised I had seen you, but I didn't put it together until this afternoon." His hand threaded through my unbraided waves.

I shut my eyes and remembered the look on his face when he picked me up off the glass-littered floor. "You look so much like him," I slowly began. "It terrified me when you saw me because I thought it was him somehow toying with me. Even after everything he did to me, I feel as though no time had passed, as if none of it matters anymore."

"Rona, would you please look at me," Cain said.

I opened my eyes, and his tenderness crushed my last resolve to pieces. He was lost, too, his loneliness so closely mirrored in my gaze.

"I thought these were contacts at first." His fingertip brushed the skin beside my eye. "They're real, aren't they?"

"Yes."

"What can you tell me?"

"Anything," I said. "I am forbidden to lie."

"What are you?"

I smiled, unwilling to tell him just how long. "I'm not sure. But I am no longer human, haven't been for a long time."

He swore under his breath, shook his head, and smiled. "That's kind of awesome, babe."

"And...this is a good thing?"

Cain laughed. "Hell yeah. When your skin started changing colors in the shower, I thought I was losing my mind for good."

"You are such a strange human." Anyone else would have already forgotten what they had seen. What made Cain so different?

"It's a well-known fact," he replied. "So, Rona the not-quite-human, why are you here?"

I grimaced through my reply. "I was drawn, called to you and Lissa. It is my duty to protect true love." Confusion clouded his aura like an opaque silver fog, so I added, "I came here to rescue your true love, Cain—yours and Lissa's."

His reaction was not what I expected. Rather than rant and rave, comprehension fell over him like a wet blanket until determination replaced his defeat. "Rona, I hate to break it to you, but I'd say it's too late for that."

"Impossible," I denied, not because I didn't agree with him. I feared losing everything all over again.

"But you don't know that for sure, do you?" He propped his head on his arm and smirked.

I turned onto my back with a huff. "I am cursed, Cain. For over two thousand years, I have been unable to feel anything but the emotions of humans I aid." I didn't add that hatred and sorrow were emotions I understood well, my constant companions.

"If that's true, can you feel this?" he asked before reaching and snatching my chin into another heated embrace.

Too soon, I pulled out of his reach. "We can't!" I pleaded, until Cain leaned forward to capture my mouth again. His hand threaded through my hair as he drew me back into his arms. All further protests came out as a moan, and this only drove his passion further. Soon it became less a mission to convince me and only a need for more touch, a stronger thrill, to feed the temptation.

I pushed forward, pressing his back to the bed as I climbed onto his waist, savoring the growing heat between us. I would have never stopped had he not pushed my hair back from my face and gently pushed me back.

His almost perfect smile was only made brighter by the contrast of his darkly bronzed skin. "You want to try telling me again you didn't feel any of that?"

I shook my head and sighed when he lowered me into his embrace. As we calmed from our most recent high, I wanted to deny him. I should make him forget me so he could find his true love. But tomorrow the snow would begin to melt. Tomorrow, Cain would return to his life and the woman he truly loved. So I would be selfish just this one night.

After he fell asleep, I lay awake in the dark and whispered the truth I couldn't admit to myself.

"I love you."

"*I loved the way he looked at me and the way he smiled. His eyes are a beautiful blue that kind of just stare right through you.*"
—ELLEN

10

AWAKENING

Overnight, the blizzard finally ceased, and the sun reclaimed the city at an exponential rate. Weather scientists were baffled by the sudden turn and blamed it on the phenomena they named global warming. I listened to the relieved sighs of the families around us. Heat meant work and money and food. For the first time in two days, horns blared outside in the streets.

I savored the steady beat of Cain's heart before leaning back to take in his sleep-softened features. I never realized how much of an effort he made to keep up his mask. Dimly dawned light was kind to his scarred face. Before the cruelty that scarred his face, he must have been considered more than handsome. His jaw was pronounced and square at the chin, dusted in the stubble he forgot to shave the day before. His lips were full and his chief tool for expression. How often had I watched those lips curve and dimple into the slightest of fond smiles? Before

I had captured his affections, I thought his mouth a harsh thin line, which I knew now he gathered together in defense. The scar which began below his neck and grooved up the side of his mouth and just shy of his eye was new.

It was the lingering pain of old wounds that made me press my lips to his collarbone. I intended to stop there with a lingering caress. But so close to the knife's trail, I could almost hear the echoes of his pain. So I traced the scar up his neck with soft kisses. Even as he stirred I continued, blinking back tears when I reached his chin and paused at the corner of his mouth.

The bare chest beneath my palms hitched, and his hands hovered over my back. Before I could lift my chin, he cupped my face and pushed me up to look at him. We breathed in time, into each other. Something shifted in his eyes as they cleared from sleep. I gasped as he rose to capture my mouth in a desperate kiss.

This is the last time…I told myself as his tongue parted my lips and drove me to new heights. When I pushed my hand against his chest for leverage, he moaned and pulled me flush against his length.

The electronic ring of his cell phone broke the haze of passion and need between us. Cain's eyes squeezed shut as he pressed his forehead to mine. I glared at the jarring piece of machinery as it continued to ring.

"Should you not pick up?" I asked, borrowing the modern phrasing. Cain ignored my question in favor of tracing the pulse at my neck with his lips. His fingers dug into my sides for one last tug before he released me with a low curse.

Cain snatched the device before lying back on his pillow.

His annoyance was replaced by dread as he read the screen and placed it to his ear. "Yeah? Oh, hey boss…okay." His gaze met mine before lingering on my tousled blond curls.

I sank back against his lap, and Cain screwed his features, battling pleasure with heated concentration.

"*Yeah,* I got it. Be there in ten," he grunted. After letting the phone slip from his hand, he sighed and threw his arm over his eyes. "That wasn't very nice," he mumbled.

"What wasn't very nice?" I innocently batted my lashes at him, unable to hide my grin.

"This," he replied.

I screeched when he leapt up, wrapped me in his arms, and then began to tickle my sides. Laughter burst from my lungs. My mouth opened wide with surprise as tears escaped my eyes because of the forgotten sensation. Was this what joy felt like?

Cain flipped us around so I was pinned beneath him.

Lingering giggles stuttered my breath until I realized his teasing fingers had stopped to grip the sheets on either side of my head. His hips dragged over mine, and I gasped as we molded perfectly together.

"Much as I would rather stay right here with you all day," he began in a playful tone, "I have to go back to work. Seems like the storm cleared up enough for them to clear the roads, and my boss doesn't like to wait." He breathed in deeply, hesitated, and I could feel the weight of things unsaid through our connection. Finally, he leaned down to taste my lips once more before rising.

No better farewell could I have dreamed of in all my hundreds of lifetimes.

I watched as Cain readied for the day. He watched me as if

he thought I might disappear any second.

He gave instruction as he rushed from room to room. "Lock up the door behind you. Don't leave for any reason, not even if someone bangs on that door screaming, you hear me? We don't need anybody asking questions until I know that guy you keep mentioning isn't coming after you. But if anything happens, you can go across the hall to my neighbor, Ms. Nguyen, for help. She's kind of adopted me and won't ask any questions."

Cain's sculpted chest was littered with scars covered by tattoos. It was a pity he had to throw on so many layers to leave the apartment. From my current vantage point, watching him dress for the day, regarding me with such affection, I had difficulty understanding why Lissa ever chose another over him.

"Club ain't opening tonight, so I should be back around five, okay?" Cain stood at the foot of his bed, fully dressed for what I knew to be grueling work. Hopefully the sun had melted enough snow and he wouldn't suffer too much.

I smiled and attempted to press assurance through our connection. "I'll be fine. I am stronger than I look."

He turned to leave, braced his weight against the doorframe with his hands, and then rapped it twice. "Okay, well I guess I'll see you later."

I nodded eagerly as I gathered my bare legs against my chest and watched his breath hitch. Cain struggled only another moment before crossing the room in three swift strides. With practiced ease, he caught me by the waist and hauled me into his arms for another heart-pounding kiss.

I didn't know if I could survive any more of these. Already I felt myself breaking into pieces at the thought of the day I would watch Lissa fall into his arms instead. The day I would be forced to walk away from him forever. So I did not waste another moment. I dragged my fingernails over his short-cropped hair and kissed him back.

"Please don't leave me," he whispered, and I nodded in agreement.

If only I could tell him the truth.

After ages spent living like a wraith, walking through walls and drifting through floors and ceilings, I wanted to try something new. Minutes after Cain left, I donned my dress and one of his smaller leather jackets for protection against the cold. After stuffing my cloak into one of the deep inside jacket pockets, I walked through the open door.

A mashed hubbub of people filtering through the building awaited me on the other side. Cain's flat was on the fourth floor, and the stairs connecting the top and lower levels were close to his door. Several people had gathered in the hall and were whispering in hushed voices, glancing about with suspicious eyes. Children chased each other up and down the stairs, and somewhere the baby we often heard was wailing.

I knew I must look crazy standing there grinning like an idiot, but it had been so long since I had *belonged* anywhere.

"You need something, sugar?"

I nearly jumped out of my skin but was more surprised I hadn't noticed the tiny woman approach until she was already standing in front of me. Her dark eyes appraised me with calculated intensity. She stood at least a head shorter than me. Her silver-streaked black hair was twisted and held in place by a scarf, and her wardrobe looked a time gone by. But there was mischief in the twist of her ruby lips. She puffed her cigarette with glee, sizing me up as if I were a brand-new doll.

"Well, you just gonna stand there all day?" She used the thickly smoking stick to point at me before taking another drag.

If anything, my smile only grew as I replied, "Ms. Nguyen right?" When the woman made no move to reply, I tried again. "Cain said you were a trusted friend."

The aged woman waved away the haze that was drifting between us and cackled. "Friends, eh? How times have changed. Used to be, only certain people willing to pay enough could call me friend. Good thing my no-good ex made me respectable, eh?"

She was brash and crude and utterly fascinating to me.

I'd always preferred to go by the rules, which meant never to let your job see you. It never occurred to me to pay attention to the others, those people you glance at briefly but pass by on the street. It was nice to speak to one of them for a change. I smiled, and Ms. Nguyen shook her head, tilting it at a curious angle.

"You sure are a strange bird," she commented. "Oh well, beggars can't be choosers! At least Cain's bringing home a new girl, finally. Could never understand how a fine fella like him refused to take up all the offers thrown his way. Because let's face it, honey, we both know he's a Grade A, prime-cut, first-class piece of bona fide *man*." Blowing a fresh stream of smoke out the corner of her mouth, she finished, "And you are just too adorably perfect to be real. Whatcha do? Bat your pretty eyes and make him swoon?" She winked at me to take the edge off her intrusive questions.

I laughed aloud, surprising and finally pleasing my temporary neighbor with this unexpected response. She nodded to herself as if deciding something.

"You alright, sugar," she said. "Knock if you need anything. Pay attention while you out there. Most of them ain't as good as Cain. Hope you know how lucky you are." And with one last flick of her cigarette, Ms. Nguyen returned to her cracked-open door, leaving nothing but a trail of ashes behind.

෨෨෨

I left the building feeling sure of myself and the human streets I walked. For the first time, I passed through not as an immortal apparition, but a slow walk among the masses. A whole new world of smells and textures had awakened in me because of my time with Cain. He reminded me what it was to feel again, of what friendship and love could be. It was bittersweet knowing my time among them would end as soon as I completed my mission. After this, I would return to the shadows and an endless existence of *being* and only feeling enough to preserve and rescue doomed love.

Was it truly wrong of me to try and savor it while I could? Was I wrong to try and snatch up as much of this freedom as I could? Seid had not appeared from the sky or called me to his palace to punish me for this indiscretion. No higher power over him had done anything to stop me.

Or stop Seid from cursing me in the first place, I bitterly reminded myself.

It took much longer for me to find Derek's high-end flat on foot than using my supernatural gifts. Part of me feared using my gift again and losing the liberty of humanity. But if I was going to make it to Lissa in time, I needed speed. Closing my eyes made it easier to see the unseen world shifting around the human city. Lissa and Cain's thread that had tied them together now hung as fragile as spiders silk.

Pushing my guilt to the bottom of my heart, I let the curse expand from that tightly bound place in my soul to trickle back into my skin. Already the bronze shades of my skin began to reflect a rainbow's array of color, and my need to be invisible had returned. At least people easily forgot me once I was gone. It reminded me of my one consolation and sorrow. In giving in to Cain, I was forced to accept how easily he would forget once I left.

ℛℛℛ

Before entering, I wrapped the cloak over my shoulders and donned the hood so it shaded my face. Derek's apartment suite was squeaky-clean, refreshed from his maid's recent buffing. Judging from the continuous high buzzing of cleaning machinery nearby, I knew the maid hadn't left.

My chin snapped to the left as I heard the click of heels on the tile. Lissa wore the same ensemble she had left the club in days before. By the confident sway of her hips and obvious meticulous primping, she had managed to gloss up better than ever. I took a step back before she knocked into me on her three-inch stilettos and watched her pause before the hall mirror. Her luscious curls spilled over her face, and her lips parted with a faint gasp. Green eyes widening in fear, she quickly reached inside her clutch and pulled out her makeup. Covering the bruise on the outside was the easy part, I wanted to tell her. What Derek had done to her wasn't something she could cover, nor *should* she have to cover it.

After twisting her neck, chin to shoulder and back again, she nodded with grim determination. "It's for the best, chica. Derek's gonna give us what we always wanted, remember?" Her voice trailed off the moment a uniformed maid peeked her face around the corner. Lissa stiffened and replaced her despair with a stronger mask. The maid watched her with disdain, hidden beneath a blank stare. The message was loud and clear.

Guilt infested me as I followed Lissa out of Derek's apartment.

It's your fault. You were selfish staying with Cain and not looking after her.

We crossed many intersections alongside hubs of people that switched streets in well-trained herds. Lissa was trying hard not to act like the looks some gave bothered her. Here was where the wealthy and powerful ruled. Even to my untrained eye, I could see she didn't fit in with this uptown crowd.

Sliding into the cab before she closed the door was more of a challenge. But it allowed me the rare opportunity to ride inside the chipped yellow vehicle. And as she twisted her fingers and picked at her nails, a wild idea began forming in my head.

"So, I guess the answer is support.
Without that, everything falls out of place."
—CLAUDIA

11

Convincing Lissa

Within an hour, we arrived back where my journey began. The club looked dead from the outside, along with the rest of this sleepy, older section of the city. Lissa pushed her hand through me to reach the door of the cab. I shuddered on contact and pushed aside the depression that lingered within me from her touch. Humans accidently brushed through me sometimes, but that was when I was less *human*. Usually, I only caught glimpses of the strongest of their emotions, not this breath-knocking, mind-reeling force of feeling.

Brushing Lissa's sorrow aside, I followed her through the door at the front of the building and down a luxurious staircase.

The club looked bright and polished in the light of electric lamps. Lissa paused at the foot of the dance floor, shifting on her heels and gripping her clutch until her knuckles turned white.

A cleaner mopped the floor between the many booths and tables lining the edge of the club. At the peak of its glory days, this place must have been dressed like a palace. Much of the original gold plating and filigree had survived, aged like perfected wine. Obvious care had been taken to preserve the old grandeur that Cain's uncle maintained. The floor space was vast, bordered by the long strip that made up the stage and the kitchens on the opposite side. At one end of the bar, a stairwell led to a side exit. The other stairwell rose to balcony. It was almost impossible to tell how far this second floor went, but it seemed the ideal place to find privacy.

A deep, booming voice startled both of us. "Analissa Sanchez! Where in God's name have you been? Chloe said something about you cozying up to Derek Vanderbilt the other night. I thought I told you to stay away from that rich bastard." The well-dressed figure that approached us had the same warm brown skin as Cain, only his was a shade darker, and his black hair was worn even closer to his head. He was beautiful in a dark and powerful way. I knew instinctively this must be Cain's cousin.

Lissa walked up to him with an easy swagger and purred while pressing a hand to his arm, "Don't be like that, boss. I didn't want to bother you. And Derek was…*there.*"

He chuckled low and kissed her hand with false tenderness. "Don't feed me more of your usual shit, baby. I'm not Cain, so I don't think you hung the moon with your cheap—assets." He waggled his eyebrows suggestively at her. Before she could protest, he continued, "Then again, now that you dumped my poor baby cousin, I doubt he'll believe a word coming out of that mouth of yours."

Lissa hugged her arms to her chest and lifted her chin in defiance. "You used to believe me too."

His laugh was sudden and pained. For the first time, I noticed the small glass in his hand when he tossed back the amber liquid. After setting it to rest on the nearby bar, he turned to face her and smirked. "You took care of that real quick, though, didn't you, baby? Taught me a lesson I'll never forget. But hey, let's not forget the rules of the game. All's fair in hate and war after all."

For the first time, I noticed a twisted, knotted, scarlet cord connecting them. I had seen all kinds of connections in the past, and the color of the cord always revealed the nature of the relationship. Never had I seen one the color of a bleeding sunset.

"God, will you ever shut up, Jude?" Lissa hissed.

"You brought it up, baby." Jude barred her path before she could walk away.

"I'm hungover and not in the mood," Lissa said with a smack to his arm.

Jude took two steps back and kept his hands raised. "Wanna know something? I don't care who you pass your time with, so long as you remember who's the boss. I'm letting you live with me, because otherwise we both know you'd just be another rat in the gutter. Lucky for you, you happen to be the best vocalist we've had in years. So how about you do us a favor and take care of yourself for a change? Try to not act like a hooker with *all* my clients, baby." With these parting words he winked before disappearing through the dark doorway he'd come from.

Lissa stood rigidly after, and if I wasn't mistaken, seemed on the verge of tears. Instantly I understood that while she attempted to be tough on the outside, she was just as vulnerable within. Women like her made it their mission to never reveal their gentle souls. Even if they were paralyzed with fear, as long as others remained oblivious, that was all that mattered. I understood because I was one of these women.

A short, balding man dragged his instrument onto the stage and began to tweak the knobs at the head of its neck. His instrument was much larger than Cain's electric guitar, more polished, and formed from solid wood rather than plastic and metal.

Lissa jumped when he began to tune the weather-strained strings. A faint smile pushed her full lips as she called out, "Yo, Nicky!" She offered a slight wave of her hand, and her posture shifted from defeat into confidence. Already she was adopting the people-pleasing mask she had perfected. Nicky, the strings player, shot her a wink and a wave back.

I followed the click of Lissa's heels to a door beside the stage, up a flight of steps, and down a burgundy-painted wall. The door she led me through revealed a dressing room, complete with light-studded mirrors and clothes strewn about the many chairs and racks. Lissa inspected the room before sitting in front of her mirror. Once she was sure she was alone, her mask fell. With great effort, she contained the trembling of her lips and the spilling of tears.

"You're okay," she soothed. "Jude may think he's got you figured out, but nobody really knows the truth, and that's how it's gonna be, chica." Finished with her pep talk, she picked up a small stick, twisted it, and applied the bright-pink paste to her lips. My eyes wandered as she covered her bruises with makeup the same shade as her bronze skin.

Her bruises made me wince, and I turned my attention to some of the other dressing tables. I carefully ran a hand over the endless bottles and cases, the brilliant sequins and bold colors of the dresses. Everything about this city radiated false beauty, yet somehow reminded me of my past. My sisters and I had been pressured into enhancing our looks in any manner we could, be it oils, spices, or superstitious remedies. Father had been so proud of my golden locks, a rare feature in our part of the world. I was his prize, and he had been attempting to sell me to the highest bidder when the god of the seas found me.

I stared so long at my reflection, I was unaware I let my cloak slip. Cain's jacket felt oppressively warm just then, yet before I could shrug it off, I realized my mistake.

Lissa gasped and barely caught a glass vial before it crashed on the ground in her haste to stand. "Hey! I—didn't think anyone else was here yet."

Shame filled me. How could I have revealed myself to her so unwittingly? Now I was more than convinced Cain was a bad influence. Could I dare speak to Lissa and expect her not to remember me after I left?

"Forgive me," I began. "I did not mean to startle you." At last I lifted my gaze to face the full brunt of her curiosity. I could sense her trying to work it out through our connection, and how she could pin me into a comfortable place. Humans always tried to write off the supernatural with some rational explanation.

A smile spread over her face as she tapped a pink, perfectly manicured fingernail to her lip. "You must be new, eh? How much did Jude offer you up front? Better have been higher than minimum wage, for what the other girls have to put up with. Word of advice, chica? Don't give him an inch, or he'll cheat you for all you're worth."

I fought the unease creeping beneath my skin the closer she came and gripped the cloak in my hands. This was the second time I had willingly broken the rules and spoke to a human. What made talking with her so different from Cain?

Maybe it's because he's wearing Seid's face? My conscience deadpanned an easy reply back to me.

When I looked up, I saw her startlingly green gaze had shifted to Cain's jacket. Seemingly unperturbed by the fact I never agreed with her previous comments, Lissa changed tactics.

"So..." She slid her hand onto the dresser table and cocked her hip to the side. "I don't think I caught your name. I'm Lissa Sanchez." She stuck her hand out into the air between us. Past her false smile and rigid posture, I saw her actions for what they were. She felt threatened.

Lissa lifted her chin to meet my eye as I rose to my feet. I was small compared to Cain. Next to Lissa, however, I was nearly a head higher, even with her heeled shoes. I knew I shouldn't have been satisfied to see the falter in her step. I hid my smirk when she squeezed my hand, only to find my grip was subtly tighter than hers. If I were as vicious as some of the gods I had known, I might have snapped her in two. Luckily for Lissa, I had never been a violent person to begin with.

"Orona," I finally replied, giving her the only name I could still remember.

The viper waiting to strike behind her smile quickly turned genuine, so quickly I nearly missed the change. "Nice stage name."

Lissa dropped my hand to inspect the rim of her nails and shifted her weight on awkwardly arched feet. How these women managed wearing high stilts, I would never understand.

"So, *Orona*, want to tell me what you're doing with Cain's jacket?"

"I—only borrowed it."

"And he actually *let* you touch it? I'm surprised…" She trailed off, waiting for me to ask her the obvious question. When she realized I wasn't taking the bait, she added, "It was his pop's."

"I'm just a friend visiting from out of town. Don't worry, I'll be leaving soon," I said and tried not to make it sound like it was rehearsed. It was partially true, after all.

Lissa's casual smile faded. "What's that got to do with me? We ain't together anymore, honey, or did he tell you different?" She caught her top lip between her teeth and added, "He didn't mention me or anything? Did he? Not that I care, you know. It's just, I like to know what my exes say about me."

"He spoke well of you, Lissa," I said with an encouraging smile.

The young woman softened as I knew she would, and the scarlet thread attached to her began to fade, while hers and Cain's golden thread flickered back to life. Hope flared the same instant a fresh ache stabbed through my chest.

"Really?" Lissa brightened. "I never would have thought he would, after…"

Guilt shadowed her aura in a gray cloud, and she was once more the frightened girl from the bathroom mirror, not this role she tried to play.

I startled as Lissa suddenly squeezed my hand. She glanced both ways down the dressing room. "I've got an idea." She snatched a nearby golden strapless dress, *if it could be considered a dress*, and pushed it into my hands.

"Here, put this on real quick!"

I didn't want to change out of my dress. I had worn it like a second skin for so long, but one look at the thinly masked desperation in Lissa's eyes, and I remembered the blood on her hands. That memory was enough for me to strip in front of her shamelessly and slip the dress overhead.

"What is this for?" If I was going to play a part like Lissa, I at least wanted to know what I was getting myself into.

"You'll see!" she cryptically replied. Primping and prodding me for another second, she then attempted to untie my sandals, to which I literally put my foot down. I refused to wear those ridiculous stilts.

Unperturbed, Lissa reached up and applied a layer of bronze paste to my lips. "There, now you're perfect. Come on. Let's ditch rehearsal," she said.

"Where are we going?"

"Girls night out." Lissa took my hand firmly in hers and pulled me back to the hall outside the dressing room. "My treat, chica. Trust me, you'll be thanking me after a few drinks."

Lissa winked, and I knew I had earned her trust, or at the least piqued her interest. Now all I had to do was convince her to reunite with the mortal I loved.

❧❧❧

The effects of alcohol on human inhibitions had not changed with the times, I noted. Timid and morose people suddenly became passionate exhibitionists after a few glassfuls of the poison. In my time, wine was in more abundance than water. Yet it had never tasted this sweet. To my surprise, the liquid didn't affect me at all.

I still remembered my wedding party, the night I ran away from my new husband and into Seid's arms. Sometimes, I wondered if the poison in my blood had made me more desperate to do whatever my lover asked of me. It certainly made my husband crueler than he'd ever been before my father's arrangement.

I had happily avoided close contact with humans for years and now remembered why. I could feel their connections to each other, accidently absorbed with wisps of their emotions and dreams. It made my mind overflow with images and the need to help fulfill these wishes. Sometimes what waited inside their souls was dark and twisted, like my husband had been before Seid killed him.

After riding in another, dirtier yellow cab and listening to Lissa rant about the nightclub and its unfair manager, Jude, we had arrived at our destination.

The club was another underground "hotspot," she insisted, only more modern.

Men leered as we passed them by and headed to the bar behind the dance floor. Music blared so loudly I thought my ears might burst, even if I was supposedly indestructible. My heart thudded in my chest in time with the beat, and I watched Lissa dance as she led us to a pair of open stools.

"Isn't this great?" she shouted over the din.

I shrugged but smiled for her sake. I wasn't here for my own pleasure, but to finish my mission. I had already been here too long, and dragging things out wasn't going to help any of us in the end.

"What'll it be?" the handsome bartender asked.

"Two Jack Daniels and Dr. Peppers, for my sister and me here."

"Ain't that a little hard for a pretty thing like you, this early in the day?"

When she batted her lashes and leaned farther over the counter, I watched his mouth tilt into an even bigger grin. "Don't worry. I'm a big girl."

Time was nonexistent in this place. People danced to their own rhythm with the transition from one song to another. Lissa basked in the male attention, in the rapid pace of the pulse-pounding music and the heat from too many bodies writhing together.

The energy of the people, the music, and the alcohol seemed to be her way of coping with the disappointment her life had become. As I sipped and Lissa downed glass after glass, more truths slipped past her lips. She told me about Cain and how he was the first to welcome her when she moved to this neighborhood.

"I convinced my abuela to take me in my last year of high school. Was looking for a ticket out of the slums. I just knew I was better than what I'd been told to expect for myself growing up. I didn't want to end up like my parents, cleaning houses and working the restaurant. I wanted to *sing*."

"You were not afraid?" I asked.

She paused mid-sip, and her shoulders shook with rich laughter. Her words began to slightly slur.

"Oh, chica, you don't even want to know what I had to do

to get where I'm at."

"So when did you fall in love with Cain?"

Stricken, Lissa gripped her drink, and tears welled in her eyes. "I didn't plan on it. He was just a means to an end. I'd known him from school, and used him to get a gig at the club. His cousin runs the place, you know. Once I got in good with Jude, I dumped Cain…sure you can figure out the rest."

"No. What happened?" I rested my head in my hand in a hopefully human gesture and waited.

"I shouldn't care what you think, but once I tell you this, you'll probably hate me. Everyone else does." Lissa took in a slow breath, then called, "Give me another, Stevo."

I waited as the bartender refilled Lissa's glass, watched her take one more drink, then listened as she finally began, "I don't know what he told you, but I really screwed things up. I live with his cousin, but Jude knows I sleep around with the clients sometimes. I left Cain because he couldn't give me what I needed. I ain't gonna be poor the rest of my life, you know. Every day, I keep thinking I'll meet the right guy, and he'll help get me where I wanna be. But now… I'm not so sure anymore."

Tears spilled past her cheeks, marking her beautiful face with black streaks as Lissa hung her head in her hands. Her rich brown hair masked either side of her face, and her words were muffled as she moaned, "—didn't mean to do it. Derek said it was the only way, you know? He's got a wife and kids outside the city. I should have known better…but he said the pills wouldn't hurt. Oh God, what if Cain finds out?"

A part of me wanted to hate her as I realized she had thrown away yet another joy I could never know. But I couldn't hate Lissa any more than I hated myself. I wished to comfort this girl, who believed she had no other choice. And though I could understand why Cain was so determined to prove he wasn't in love with Lissa, I wished to give her hope. Why else had I been drawn to them in the first place?

Lissa not-so-discreetly wiped her face with a napkin from the bar before lifting her head and pasting a bright smile on her face. "Clearly we've heard enough of my sorry past. What did Cain say about me? You mentioned good things?"

I hesitated then offered the truth I was compelled to share. "He tries to hide his feelings for you still, but he hasn't forgotten."

"I bet he hasn't." She frowned at the water ring her glass left on the bar. "But I think it's too late for us."

At her admission, part of me longed to run home to Cain and throw my worries to the wind. The wind and the sea and the storm were Seid's domain, and I wanted nothing to do with him or the gods any longer. I just wanted Cain.

But I could not banish the memory of Lissa doubled over in Derek's bathroom. Or her confession of what she'd sacrificed.

I should have been the mortar that would mold Cain and Lissa together. Instead I was the wedge driving them further apart.

"Orona? You all right?" Lissa nudged me gently with her elbow. "You obviously ain't from around here, chica. Thinking in your first language? I do it all the time. And I swore after I left home I wasn't using Spanish no more."

Her giggle sounded too false to my ears.

"You've had a lot to drink." I motioned to the empty glasses.

Lissa shrugged, oblivious to my inner turmoil. "Oh, this is nothing. Come on! We're two caliente mamas, and we need to dance!"

I followed her because I knew this was what she needed.

Soon enough, we had two male partners pressed up against us. I followed the beat and found an ancient rhythm hidden in this modern dance. Giving in, I closed my eyes and fell deeper into the steps.

I could almost see my sisters twirling with their veils and scarves around the fire, coaxing Father's guests to join. I saw Father discussing my future with the most powerful man in the city. And when I turned my back to the fire, to face the crashing waves, Seid's maelstrom eyes waited for me.

Lissa's laughter drew me into the present, to her glazed-over green gaze and the undulations of a stranger dancing against my back. Disgust filled me as he slipped his hand to the inside of my exposed thigh.

"Do not touch me!" I pushed him roughly away. Several people gasped as the man went careening into them. My blood ran too hot, rising along with the beginnings of my gift.

I fled back to the safety of the bar and struggled to push the need to fade, to disappear beneath a calmer pulse.

It was stupid to have followed Lissa today. I didn't belong here, dancing with strangers, any more than she did. Lissa put on a good show, presenting the persona she thought people needed while ignoring her deeper needs. But I had been around far too long to be fooled and saw her carefully concealed tender heart.

She proved this to me the moment she followed me off the dance floor and took my hand in hers. "You okay, chica? You don't look so good. Want me to have Stevo call you a cab?"

"You don't mean to come with me?" I dared.

Lissa glanced over her shoulder at the handsome stranger smiling back at us. "No, I'm good here. Stevo always keeps an out for me, so no worries."

"What about Cain?"

Her joy faded, but her smile didn't dim as she ignored my question.

"You know, I was jealous earlier when I saw his jacket on you. But you're all right, Rona. Just..." Lissa squeezed my hand then added, "Don't make the same mistakes I made."

"And then, real love I think comes later. When you really get to know someone and how they think and feel, when you can't imagine if something were to happen to them. When you trust them and want to spend all your time doing nothing with them, when you want to grow old together."
—MELISSA

12

POSSESSION

The first time I breathed underwater was in his arms. As long as I was with Seid, no storm or tempest could harm me. His home beneath the waves was more beautiful than anything I could have imagined, a pearl-crafted palace of light. Poseidon was always a being of such contrasting natures, light and dark, beauty and ugliness. I loved all of him.

Eventually, I grew used to the gills he placed on my neck and chest that allowed me to breathe with him in the depths. We spoke with our minds as if it were the most natural thing in the world. It was there I asked him of his life before I entered it. Had he ever known true love before?

"No," he replied, stroking the inner skin of my arm. "You are the first and the last, Orona. My brothers have chosen different paths, and I always thought them fools. I know what your legends say, but in truth, I was never tempted long enough to fall for a mortal. You have become my undoing."

He covered my mouth with his, and the air escaped us in thick shining spheres that floated above.

In the end, I chose not to get in the cab. I needed time to think, and my connection to Cain would bring me home soon enough. Or so I thought.

My walk back to Cain's apartment was not pleasant in the thin dress Lissa had loaned me. My other dress and cloak were back in the dressing room I had been whisked away from. I wondered at the state of my mind, that I could forget what had become my second skin. In Lissa's haste to dampen her somber spirits, I had forgotten myself. Now I wished for that mind-numbing chill that made men seek shelter and the heat of a warm fire.

My day with Lissa had been charged with drinks, dancing, and human delights, yet only a familiar emptiness lingered. Ignoring the stares and occasional calls from the people I passed, I gave my will to the pull Cain had over me and followed it home.

By the time I neared his street, my hair was covered in snow, and the sandals covering my feet did little to battle the freeze. It shouldn't have affected me. Was I truly naked and powerless without my cloak, or was this something more?

Worst of all, I didn't know how to repair the wounds Lissa had inflicted on Cain. True, I did not know his part in their story yet. But I could see nothing but goodness in him. If the child had been Cain's, how could she have destroyed it without Cain's say in the matter? Lissa's logic confused me as much as her naivety incited my compassion.

"What do I do now, Seid?" I glared up at the heavens. This was the danger of giving in to mortal emotions. When the bitterness faded away, nothing but a never-ending ache remained. I clutched my gold-sequined slip and tried to ignore the sting in my heart.

"I still hate you…" I whispered to the cool night air.

Closer to Cain's apartment, the streets were far less crowded and the house lights of hardworking citizens already extinguished. In some cases, the artificial lights would burn till dawn, until their workload was completed. When I checked the position of the stars, I realized how late it was and picked up my pace.

Forgetting the eyes of mortal men, I reluctantly tapped into the curse and allowed its power to expand. I willed the winds to pull me as I gave into it, for my body to be weightless and the world to rush past the final block to Cain's building.

His motorcycle was gone from its metal post. Residual feelings of fear and panic lingered in the air where his vehicle had been.

I blamed the alcohol for my lack of foresight. I knew Cain should have been home some time ago. But what if the curse had made him forget about me already?

"Where could he have gone?" I asked, already knowing the answer.

From here, I could hear the voices inside his apartment building as they spoke of Cain's new girlfriend. They said the lonely biker had knocked on the doors of thieves, drug dealers, and ordinary people, asking after *me*.

Though I shouldn't have worried about the human, I rushed back onto the street. I was an indestructible and immortal being, so worry and shock had long ago fled my makeup.

I turned toward the screech of tires on ice and the rumble of a heavy engine's approach. I froze before the bold headlight blinded me. The pain in my chest eased the closer he sped to me.

Cain's bike groaned and slid in a precarious circle until his body was nearly parallel to the asphalt. At the last possible moment, he thrust out a clunky black boot to catch his fall.

"Rona!" Cain stripped off his helmet and killed the engine but forgot the headlight in his haste to reach me. "Do you have any idea what I thought when I came home and you weren't there? And after I *told* you to stay put!"

I held my ground even as he advanced upon me. His blue eyes were brilliant against his brown skin, his body a silhouette before the artificial headlight.

I couldn't help smiling as he grasped my arms and held me in place as his warmth infected me. I hadn't known I was freezing until he held me. I didn't know until then, after the long hours of separation, that with Cain I could pretend to be human.

Now that I knew the pain Lissa had put him through, I wondered how Cain could still carry so much love in his heart. Rather than uttering meaningless words, I slipped my arms about his neck and buried my face in his chest. A feeling greater than happiness wrapped around me, and the unfulfilled emptiness within me filled to the brim.

Cain snatched me up as if I weighed nothing and crushed me to his chest until I was no longer trembling with cold.

Silence separated us as he returned his bike to its resting place and carried me to his apartment. Ms. Ngyuen watched us from the open crack in her doorway and smiled knowingly at me when our eyes met.

Cain's work clothes were scattered, and the apartment was a mess. It looked as if he had taken his anger out on some of his less-than-favored furniture, including the magical couch. His mouth tightened when he noticed the direction of my attention.

"It was stupid for you to go walking out in that cold dressed like that," Cain growled as he carried me to his room. "Why were you wandering in the streets, huh? Are you asking to get killed?"

I reached out to touch his face as Cain set me down atop the sink counter in his bathroom and stripped the nearest towel off its hook. With a start, I realized this was the same towel he'd wrapped me inside the morning things changed between us.

A tiny warning flashed at the back of my mind, heralding something far more insurmountable was coming. But all I could think of was calming the dark cloud of swirling emotions covering my human's aura.

"I was in no danger, Cain," I said, hopefully assuring him. "I am much stronger than I appear." I willed him to feel the truth behind my words. He knew I wasn't normal, that I could not feel the things other people felt. And there was power stirring in him too. I had felt it all along, but only now began to wonder, as he reluctantly met my gaze, if there was not more to this mission than I was aware.

"Rona, you don't know! Didn't you say something about your powers getting weaker? How do you know some bum off the street didn't see you and decide to start some shit?"

Despair and fury oozed from his aura, overshadowed by his desperate need for control. I had seen this need before in people who had experienced too much loss, too young. Only one cure existed for such internal scars.

Cain continued to rub my shaking limbs down with the towel. Finally, his movements slowed, and his fear abated. He furrowed his brow as he tossed the towel aside and fumbled with the tassels of my skirt. "Where did you find this getup, anyway?"

The sleeve slipped off my shoulder, exposing the tattoos above my breasts that marked my lineage. "Lissa let me borrow it," I said, unthinking. "She took me out for drinks, for fun." I regretted my words the instant his expression froze into a hard-hearted mask.

"And how did you meet her, huh?" Cain demanded and then shook his head. "Unbelievable…can't believe you went to the club after I told you to leave it alone."

With a frustrated sigh, Cain stood and stripped out of his heavy coat. Forgotten muscles in my stomach clenched as I watched his shirt ride up his torso. He linked his fingers over the top of his head and hissed a stream of unintelligible phrases as he stomped out of the bathroom.

Cain sank heavily on the edge of his mattress and pulled his wet boots off. "Rona, I get it that you feel like it's your *mission* to get us back together, but I'd rather you stayed away from Lissa. She's no good for anyone. She *uses* people, Rona. No doubt she used you as her wingman to find out what I've been up to."

I hopped off the counter and walked into his space, until I stood between his parted knees. He swallowed hard as I rested my hands on his bare shoulders. "She didn't use me," I insisted. No one *used* me, not for the last two thousand years. "I simply wanted to know her. The curse brought me to both of you. I needed to learn why. And I cannot learn if I am always here with you."

I held my breath as Cain's hands slid up my thighs to clasp my hips and pull me closer. The center of his eyes darkened so the blue reflected the eye of a storm. "Did you dance with anyone tonight?"

Smiling softly, I teased him. "One or two, perhaps…" I squealed as he tipped back onto the bed then rolled until he had me effectively pinned beneath.

"Dressed like this?" He glanced down and waggled his eyebrows.

I nodded. "Do you object?"

"Not to sound too much like a caveman, but there's only one person I want you dancing with from now on."

"Who?"

His hand fisted the back of my dress as he drew me in closer and answered my question in the waves of his passion.

"I don't think you can identify any one simple thing that causes you to fall in love with someone. If they could, they'd have bottled it and sold it."
—FARLEIGH

13

Lessons in Humanity

I woke with the sun shining on my face and Cain's soft eyes hovering above me. The golden rays cast everything in a new light. The same smooth jazz music we had danced to the other day was already playing from his stereo box. The music reminded me of the club and Lissa's drunken confession the night before. How could I heal a relationship that was so obviously beyond repair?

The temptation to grumble at Seid for sending me to resurrect a lost cause was growing daily. And I had avoided speaking directly to him since he stopped appearing to me a thousand years before.

"I don't wanna leave this bed today." Cain's soothing voice washed over me as he ran a warm, calloused hand over my bare back. "I hate that I have the late shift at the club. But maybe you'd want to come to work with me?"

"Are you certain?" Tonight would grant the perfect

opportunity to bring Cain and Lissa together.

Already the thought of leaving him, of making them both forget me, was painful.

Cain pressed his thumb to my lip, releasing it from my teeth. "Rona, I know you think you still have some job to do. But haven't you stopped to think maybe we were supposed to meet? Maybe it never was me and Lissa you were supposed to hook up." The rest he left open to my overanalytical mind. Yet with his lips and hips pressed to mine, it was difficult to think of anything.

∽∽∽

A few hours after Cain left for his construction job, Mrs. Nguyen invited me to eat what she called "brunch."

Today I had decided to obey his wishes to stay in the apartment. I'd spent the morning tearing myself apart on the inside, trying to decide what was right and wrong, and learned I was not capable of the task. Truthfully, I had never been required to think this hard about what my couple needed most. Before, it was an easy fix of testing their trust or sending disaster their way to determine the power of their love. I could let the curse use me to follow through its purpose, albeit grudgingly.

Maybe it never was me and Lissa you were supposed to hook up.

Cain's words had stirred a secret hope in my chest. He knew little of the events leading up to my curse, but perhaps he was right. The curse seemed weaker in his presence, and left me feeling too human.

"You need to eat some more, honey." Mrs. Nguyen's

admonishment broke my reverie like a slap to the wrist.

"Don't see why the boys and gals today like 'em thin as a toothpick. Maybe boys feel like less of a man, need less of a girl," she cackled.

The food was mouthwatering and unlike anything I'd tasted in my immortal life. I ate as slowly and politely as I knew how, but it was hard to pretend I wasn't enjoying the meal as much as Mrs. Nguyen's company.

My eyes wandered over the rich dressings of her apartment. She had covered the cracked walls with gorgeously patterned silks. Incense burned in a corner, and her box-shaped record player crooned the same jazzy music that Cain was so fond of.

Mrs. Nguyen, who never gave me another name to call her by, had managed to keep hold of the things she loved most in life. She lived by her own code, and as that required her to listen to her heart, in many ways it was the best thing anyone could do.

Over my next mouthful, Mrs. Nguyen's onyx eyes narrowed as she took a longer drag from her cigarette. "So, you were gone for a long time yesterday. Should have seen your man, banging on the doors of neighbors he hasn't talked to in months. Not since *she* moved out, anyway."

I tensed at the mention of Lissa but held Mrs. Nguyen's gaze. She was a perceptive human, and for this reason, I trusted her.

"I went to visit Lissa," I said between bites.

"Ha!" The old lady cackled and released a stream of white smoke. She brushed her finger along one persistently loose fake eyelash. "Course you did. Have to size up the competition, eh?"

Winking, Mrs. Nguyen poured me another glass of Merlot. I sipped slowly, remembering the effects of modern alcohol on

Lissa.

"I do not bear her ill will," I replied and willed my voice free of doubts. "She and Cain belong together."

Did she go back to Derek last night, or Jude?

Mrs. Nguyen snorted into her glass before tossing back a strong dose and sighing into her curved leather seat. "That piece of candy doesn't know what she wants. But let me tell you, Mrs. Nguyen sees more than she says. And that girl was a tough dish for Cain to swallow. Always carrying on about what they needed, what *she* needed. Did she ask him what he wants? No! All about her, and that poor boy still somehow found a way to love her."

I understood this selfless love, for I had loved Seid even in his darkest hours. Even as he cursed me and we rode upon a fine line between ardor and abhorrence. In so many ways, my god had been every woman's dream. But his passion could easily turn into selfish cruelty. He claimed it was part of his nature, to be turbulent as the storm.

If Cain loved Lissa as I had loved Seid, then it was certain the truth of his love lingered beneath his pain. I only needed to find a way to resurrect it.

 софо

After brunch, Mrs. Nguyen broke Cain's orders by dragging me to her favorite old Chinatown haunts. Her words gave me, for the first time, a true glimpse into the human condition. Humanity had always been forced to circumvent its past failures. History may have given ample lessons to the present generation, yet they seemed ignorant of themselves and their past. Few cared to learn from the mistakes of fallen empires, however. They thrived off what they knew—hunger, hardship, and hope.

Cain's neighbor had no idea she was teaching me any of this, of course. Mrs. Nguyen was telling me about her past and present, of the family who barely spoke to or acknowledged her and the husband she never forgot.

"Old age ain't your friend in America, sugar," she said as we browsed through a vendor's shop laden with meaningless items.

I paid little heed to the paper and coin she exchanged for clothes and jewelry. We had been forced into the back corner of the shop, hidden behind a curtain leading into a musty room.

Some things had not changed, apparently. The sort of bartering Mrs. Nguyen thrived on was something I recalled from my human life. Only this time, instead of coin or trade, they preferred paper.

"Why do your children not visit you?" I asked once we were outside and headed back down the road we came.

Mrs. Nguyen grasped my hand in hers and squeezed. At first I wondered if she needed comfort, but when I turned to look down, she was reaching for the wadded bills she had slipped to me when we went inside the little shop. "Hand it over, kiddo. That's some of my hard-earned cash."

"My apologies," I said and bowed my head low, afraid I had offended her. Her laughter startled me, and her eyes were shining when I met her gaze. I often did things that amused her, beyond my comprehension.

"There!" She chuckled and poked my arm. "That is why they no longer visit, think I'm too stingy with my money. But they never want to be reminded of how I got my dough in the first place. So I make sure to remind them, of course. See why they don't want to hang around me?" She laughed again but could not disguise the flash of pain that filled her eyes or the darkness clouding her aura.

☙☙☙

When we returned home, I let Mrs. Nguyen dress me in the clothes she had bought for me. I let her sit me on her vanity seat where she could paint my kohl around my eyes and on lashes.

"What lovely eyes you have, duckie. That's why you are on the run, eh? Some lab experiment gone wrong?"

"You learned my secret," I replied with a smile as Mrs. Nguyen began arranging my waist-length curls.

For a time, we listened to the record playing in the background, and my thoughts brewed like one of Seid's tempests. "Have you ever been tempted to do the wrong thing, even if it felt right?" I finally asked.

Mrs. Nguyen's smile turned vicious. "Too few people ever know true joy in life, Orona. Would it be so bad to grab happiness when fate drops it in your lap?"

"I acted for so long on instinct, with no thought as to whether my actions were right or wrong. I have forgotten what it means..."

To be human, I silently added.

Mrs. Nguyen placed her perfectly manicured nails to my chin and tilted my head to meet her appraisal. "The answer has been in front of you all along, sugar. You just got to be willing to look at things with new eyes sometimes. And keep in mind, Cain's got a say in this too."

My lips parted in surprise. Perhaps there was more to Mrs. Nguyen than the gift of discernment.

Before I could question her further, a heavy fist pounded on the apartment door.

"Mrs. Nguyen?" Cain's voice called from the other side. "Rona better be in there with you!"

I was taken aback by the fear and anger in his tone. Through the door, I glimpsed the silvery thread extended between us stretching, grasping to touch.

Mrs. Nguyen winked at me before practically dancing to the door. "Relax boy-o! I got your woman right here," she called. No sooner had she unbolted the many locks and chains than Cain brushed past her, eyes roving her den.

I peeked about the corner and pressed my fingers into the wood grain on the bathroom doorway to ground my flighty emotions.

Cain looked as though he'd had a rough day at work. Grit clung to his pores, though I could see he had attempted to wipe most of it away. What surprised me was how much I wanted him to find me and kiss me senseless anyway.

"You took her out today?" Cain plucked up a stray plastic bag and wadded it in his hand.

"Now it's a crime to keep a lonely old woman company, is it?" Mrs. Nguyen attached a fresh cigarette to the tip of a long black stem and lit the end with a match. "That's always been your problem, boy. You hold on too tight to things so they can't leave you."

Cain threw the wadded plastic away and grumbled under his breath, "Crazy old bat…"

Our hostess busied herself with changing out records and mumbled something about "ungrateful child."

I muffled a laugh behind my hand and froze when his gaze locked with mine across the room. Cain's lips turned up into a smile, the scar that marked his chin keeping one corner of his mouth lower.

"Rona? Why are you hiding back there, babe?" Cain crossed the small living area to my hiding place. His hands slipped to my waist, and his forehead pressed to mine before I could step from the doorway. "You can't keep making me worry like that. Leave a note at least next time, okay?"

"Okay," I agreed.

Cain's smile froze, and his grasp on my waist tightened as he pulled back. His eyes widened as they fixed on my face then traveled lower. "Rona, you look—" He paused for another breath. "Beautiful."

"Told you he'd love it, sugar." Mrs. Nguyen puffed away suddenly beside us and totally unfazed by the ardor in Cain's eyes.

I smiled into the eyes of my beloved, the man I wanted so desperately to keep. "Do you love it?"

Tipping my chin up with a finger, Cain replied, "Yeah."

*"We were two different people, and as strongly as we felt about each other,
we wanted completely different things from life, and it tore us apart."*
— KAITLYN

14

All that Jazz

*I*n my memories, Poseidon was terribly beautiful, his features too wild to be pleasing to the eye. Yet something in his stormy gaze drew me to him.

He chased me along our sandbar, the crashing waves our music, my heartbeat the percussion. "You cannot run forever, Rona!" he teased.

I glanced back over my shoulder to discover him nearly upon me and pushed my feet faster on the wet sand. Soon I would leave the sandbar for the sea, but I refused to let him catch me.

The tips of his fingers grazed my side, and I shrieked as I ran faster, until the wet sand didn't feel like grain between my toes.

The waves washed over my feet, and I paused to look about. I was farther out in the ocean than I had realized.

The waves calmed about my feet so as I looked down, I could see fish swimming in the deep.

Seid laughed as he slipped his hands about my waist and began to tickle my sides.

"Seid, stop it! I am going to fall!"

His smile arrived with the sun through the clouds and cast the sea around us with an infinite reflection of precious jewels. "Why do you fear when you know I will always catch you?" he said.

I melted into his kiss and knew this to be the nearest thing to paradise I could ever envision.

My foot tapped of its own free will to the music being played by the band on stage. With my eyes closed, I could almost hear the sound of the waves on that beach and how they had played chorus to our lovemaking. I could almost hear the way *his* voice sounded as he sang to me. Music had been different in my time, but the emotions hidden beneath those songs remained the same as their musical descendants.

Echoes of the past always left me with an ache I could not appease.

Upon opening my eyes, I found surroundings far cruder than my memories. The area behind the stage curtains was nothing more than a narrow strip leading down a flight of stairs that flattened into a hall which bled to the dressing rooms. I had been waiting here, savoring the hubbub of humanity without the frustration of drinking in their emotions. With Cain so near, my gift was thankfully dulled, and for the first time in ages, I could control it. If I had known turning the switch on and off could be so simple as associating with a human, I might have broken the rules long ago.

Avoiding bumping into people was nearly impossible, I'd quickly discovered once Cain deposited me backstage. To avoid the flow of traffic, I leaned against the brick wall behind the curtain and wrapped my arms over the yellow silk dress Mrs. Nguyen gifted me.

Music was constantly playing, alternating between loud and brassy, to soft and crooning.

Cain's cousin was host for the evening and made sporadic announcements into the microphone between what the musicians called "sets." His voice echoed from the speakers as the previous song drifted to an end.

"Now, I know you've all enjoyed hearing Mitch croon the greats. But tonight, we've got a special treat for you from one of our own…"

Turning my attention from his words to peek through the curtains, I searched for Cain at the entrance. When we'd first set off for the club, Cain had been so excited. He had regaled me with stories of the famous people who had played and sang there in the past. Yet something shifted in his demeanor the moment the club was in sight. A steady trickle of early customers had been seen making their way in. Cain's mask had shifted back in place at the sight of them with an added edge to his every look and word.

He had been nervous the moment we walked inside, keeping me wrapped tightly against him until we made it backstage. No sooner had he deposited me than my instructions were given.

"Stay here, but try not to get too involved. If Jude corners you, just remind him he owes me a favor." And then he'd been off to begin his guard duty.

I was good at being invisible, even when forced to be more human. At the moment, I was ignoring Jude, trying to answer my own questions of what was right and wrong. Until I knew the answer to that, I was not going to force Cain and Lissa back together.

As if I had summoned her, the diva herself appeared from the dressing room in a flurry of sequins and painted-on glamour. Her dark curls were clipped to the side by a bejeweled clasp, her lips painted red. She paused atop the steps, clutching her stomach as her features contorted in pain. After regaining her composure, she nodded to herself and lifted her emerald eyes. She sauntered past me, unseeing, and took in a deep breath before emerging before the glaring lights.

Cheers and whistles greeted her as she spoke into the microphone. Strings were plucked, and the piano keys played the intro to her song.

"This one's dedicated to the love of my life."

Silence fell during Lissa's dramatic pause. I caught my breath, afraid of what she might say.

"That's right, I'm talking about you, Mr. Mason." She extended a finger to the audience, and an elderly man laughed loudly in turn.

I released the breath I hadn't known I was holding. Perhaps Lissa was not the terrible person Mrs. Nguyen perceived her to be. I smiled at the way Mr. Mason's aura bubbled a happy yellow.

Her voice slipped into the beginnings of her sultry song.

My invisibility skills must not have been as good as I thought, because a voice barked at me, as though he only just saw me standing behind him.

"What's she doing back here?"

Jude had found me. His dark eyes seemed to blaze at me in

the dim light backstage, and I blanched at the force behind his aura. Tempests waged war in the cloud over his head so fitfully, I could almost feel the gust of his hidden fury an arm's length away.

"Hey, miss, no one gets to lie down on the job around here. Don't you know you've only got five minutes before the next chorus number?" Cain's cousin stepped closer to me while glaring at the old man in charge of the curtain and props hidden behind it.

"You are Cain's cousin?" I asked breathlessly, reeling from the sudden assault of his emotions. I should not have let my guard down. Just the strain from reading his aura but not embracing the curse fully left me sick to my stomach. Still, the farther apart I was from Cain, the easier it became to tap into, and the less *real* I felt.

Jude crossed his arms over his finely tailored clothes as a slow smirk eased his features. "Oh, I see," he soothed. "You're Cain's new girl or something? Must say I'm impressed. Never thought my little cuz would get over that witch, and you've managed in less than a week." He thumbed over his shoulder at the stage, now being filled with so soulful a tune, it evoked my compassion.

"Lissa is not a spell caster," I said with conviction. "Her talents are of her own merit. She has shown you her natural gifts, yet you blame her for not living to your expectations."

Jude laughed and shook his head. "You don't want to make that kind of bet with me, blondie. Lissa may have convinced you she's your friend, but there's nothing behind that mask of hers, just a soulless monster."

Beyond the curtain, the crowd clapped and cried for more.

"You speak as if you have a right to judge them," I replied, angered that the human could be so blinded by his jealousy and bitterness. Was this their curse, then, to cling to their woes and never know true joy? No wonder my efforts to save them were failing.

Dark energy tumbled with electric fury over our heads and dissipated entirely as Jude advanced. "You don't know what she did to Cain. He doesn't even know the whole story. Don't let her poison your mind, blondie. I'd hate to see my little cuz get burned like that again."

"Orona?" Lissa gasped and pushed Jude out of her way before throwing her arms around my middle. Over her shoulder, I saw Jude's smug grin and was tempted to smash it off his face with my fist.

Lissa interrupted that train of thought when she pulled back with a squeal. "I can't believe Jude let you skip rehearsals and everything. But you *know* you're supposed to do this next number instead of me, remember? Like we talked about?"

I wondered why her voice sounded so strange, until she winked and the light bulb hanging behind us reflected in her olive-green eyes. I was saved from replying when she turned back to her employer.

"Oh, Jude," she began with a saccharine smile, "they're just going to love her, aren't they?"

A silent battle of wills occurred between them. While I couldn't see Lissa's expression, I watched as Jude's mouth twisted in a daring smirk. Finally, he turned back to the stage and walked out to introduce the next act.

"Lissa?" I pressed my fingertips to her bare shoulder and

flinched when she whipped round to snatch my hands in hers. I was unprepared for the tears gleaming in her eyes.

"Do me this one favor, and I swear I'll never embarrass you like this again. But you do know he would have fired your cute ass if you didn't have a better cover story. And honestly, where *were* you during rehearsals? I mean, Jude can forgive a lot of things, but he hates freeloaders."

"What shall I do?" I asked, at a loss.

"I saw what you did at the club, remember? Just *dance*," she replied as if she knew something I was not privy to.

"All the way from an exotic land, I give you our very own Olympic Pearl!" Jude led his audience in a round of applause.

Lissa pushed me forward by my shoulders. "That's you! You're on! Don't worry, I know you're gonna do great, chica!"

Jude walked past me as I entered the stage. I could tell by his dark chuckle that this was revenge for what I had said earlier. Unlike Lissa, he knew I wasn't working for him tonight.

The curtain snapped shut, and I slowly turned to face the crowd. My vision blurred under a force of white lights. I lifted a hand to shadow my gaze and waited until the crowd quieted. A few patrons coughed after as I lowered my hand again.

I sensed Cain's eyes and confusion from here. White-hot-lightning anger was building from the swirl of his aura. Somehow, I sensed he knew who had been behind this.

Just dance.

Fingering the fringe of the shawl draped over my shoulders, I took comfort in the rich texture and allowed it to drop. The first drumbeat struck when I bent to catch it. I lifted my chin again on the second. Slowly, as a rhythm began to take place, I uncurled my back and shut my eyes. Rotating my hips, I moved the shawl to twirl around me and held it up to cover part of my face.

The drums continued to play, along with the pluck of the strings, and soon I was no longer blinded by a dozen bright lights.

I was illuminated by the large fire as I danced with my sisters, hoping to please Father's important guests. Tonight was to be the night I met the merchant I was to marry, and I was determined to please him. I singled him out in the crowd, focused my gaze on him, and conveyed my intent. The heat from the flames was driving my pulse wild, and then as I blinked, beneath the weight of his lust, I began to spin even faster.

My hair whipped around my head, coming loose of its binds as I twirled faster and faster. I felt freer in that moment than all the years I had lived as a ghost to this world, until the music abruptly ceased and I dropped in a heap upon the ground. When I opened my eyes again, I stared into a sea of bright lights filled with shouts and cheers.

I burned with shame when I realized what I had done. That particular dance was not meant for just anyone, and those who would have known its meaning were long gone. In the blink of an eye, the roar of applause, I recognized all I had truly lost.

Because I chose Seid and this shadow life instead of a real one.

No one appeared on stage to usher me away, so I scrambled to my feet as quickly as I could, eager to escape. I ignored the temptation to fade away, to give into my curse.

Before I could make it down the steps to the dressing room, Jude and Lissa grabbed hold of me. I winced at the jarring sound of their voices as they talked over one another.

"How did you learn to do that, chica? You had all those men drooling halfway through that sexy ethnic thing! Even Jude here was…"

"Never mind what I was," Jude interrupted. "You do realize what this means, don't you?" He flashed me a quick grin. "I seriously hope you've got your visa, blondie."

Lissa rolled her eyes and shoved Jude aside. "Get out there, big boss, before they start eating each other."

Now that it was just the two of us, Lissa dropped her mask in favor of a genuine smile. "Told you to trust me. Stick with me, and you'll go places. If you have enough balls, you can do anything." She giggled and tugged me down into the dressing room. "Come on! Jude's already decided you got a permanent gig here. You couldn't see those guys under those lights, but we did. We are in the money, baby!"

I stumbled when she pulled me into a room of illuminated mirrors and half-dressed girls. Several of them called out as we passed.

"What took you so long!"

"Yeah, we were supposed to be on five minutes ago."

"Look what the slut dragged in."

The redhead next to Lissa's dresser threw her stick of paste against the mirror. "Good job, *Lissa*. The whole dump is love with her now. How do you expect us to top that?"

Lissa rolled her eyes and called, "Ladies, this is Jude's new girl and *my* new bestie. Any of you backstabbing hoes so much as breathe at her wrong, I'll make your lives hell. Don't think I won't."

Another girl finished tying the straps of her shoe and said,

"Yes, your highness! We know who's the favorite around here."

Their words flew overhead while I searched for the cloak I had left behind. Why had I not sought it out immediately?

You were afraid, the voice in my head taunted.

I clenched my jaw and pushed the voices in and out of my head aside. I could care less about these humans' rivalry or jealousy. From the instant I had taken my cloak off my shoulders, my keen judgment had degraded to an all-time low. I needed to remember who I had become, not who I was before.

"Hey!" Jude pushed his head through the opening. "Does this place look like a charity to you? Get out there before they tear the band apart."

Jude's girls grumbled and groaned as they obeyed, filing out of the room in a flurry of clicks until Lissa and I were alone. I felt her eyes following me as I picked up items and searched through piles of costumes for my cloak.

"What's with the freak-out, chica?" she gently asked. "Listen, the others talk tough, but they're harmless. No one's gonna hurt you, now you got us. We're a family." Her words faded to a whisper, drawing my full attention.

I glared up at Lissa, resentful of the position she'd put me in. Yet something in her words tugged at my conscience until the reason behind everything became instantly clear. Exhaling a shaky sigh, I replied, "And what about the family you started with Cain?"

Lissa gasped as if she had been slapped. "How did you know about that? N-no one's supposed to know about that! Did *he* tell you?" From the incredulity I sensed through our bond, I knew this was the last thing she'd expected. Yet this was the closest thought in her heart.

For the first time, I felt every single day of my two thousand seven hundred and eighty-eight years. And I wondered at all the times I had obeyed Seid's compulsion over me. Over the last age, I'd forced myself to grow distant to their pain and emotions. I had blamed the curse for stealing my ability to feel. But what if it was not the curse that stole my heart away? What if I had tucked my ability to feel so deeply within, I'd invented my own cage?

For the first time in my recent memory, I longed to call out to Seid for answers.

Lissa had grown even more agitated when I offered no answer. My cares went far beyond her or the man we loved. I watched her, mystified as she sank to the empty seat beside me and crumpled into herself. Tears of frustration washed the paint around her eyes into ugly streaks.

"I can't believe he told you…" she whispered bitterly. All kinship she had claimed with me earlier seemed to have evaporated into thin air. This broken shell of a young woman held no kindness in her eyes.

Perhaps Cain was right, and she only wanted to use me to be close to him?

Silent tears dripped from Lissa's chin and soiled her dress. She rubbed her palms against her cheeks and turned to a mirror to wipe the last of the kohl streaks. "I have to sing another number after the girls are done." Cursing, she added, "Can't believe I trusted you."

Trusted me?

Lissa paused to glance at me and, to my confusion, smiled. "Maybe it's 'cause you're different from the rest of us. That's why he picked you, ain't it?"

Lissa faced her reflection and touched the fading bruises her tears had unmasked. Her hands fumbled over her cosmetic cases as she rushed to hide the evidence again. "He wanted someone *pure* and smart. Fine with me," she said with a shrug and dab of a brush to her cheeks. "You can keep him."

I frowned and leaned forward, until Lissa could no longer ignore my stare, and said, "You had a chance at true joy, the kind no one could take away from you. Why did you destroy your child, when you long for a family more than anything?"

Lissa's eyes fell shut, and she shook her head. "I suppose that's what Cain told you. But it's a lot more complicated than that." Absently, she rested a hand to her womb and breathed in shakily.

"Cain did not tell me about your child," I said.

"But Cain's the only one who knew for sure before I let Derek hook me up with the pills… How could you—" Lissa's eyes widened, and underneath her fierce expression, I could almost see the girl she still was.

"I just know," I replied.

We observed one another, Lissa, with her fears, and me, with the realization of a truth I had ignored for so long. What made them human was the very reason I was cursed in the first place.

Our immortality alone did not make us inhuman. It was our fear of opening up again, of learning to love again. In a way, this made gods the most human of all. Loving me had made Seid unable to rule over the waves and storms. For that short span of time in the ancient past, I had grounded him and loosened his control.

Lissa needed more from me than selfishness. For her sake, I couldn't afford to be a covetous immortal.

I had a choice, to either snap their connection forever or lose the one thing I had left to love.

Lissa flinched as I covered her hand with mine. "No one can condemn you for the choice you made without him."

Fresh tears spilled down her cheeks, and her lips parted as she squeezed my hand, the beginnings of a smile on her face.

The dressing room door burst open behind us, shocking us with the man we'd been discussing. The man who had been born with Seid's face.

"Lissa." Cain growled out her name as he stalked toward us.

What frightened me was not his anger, but the fact he hadn't looked at me since he walked in the room.

"You have to know when to say what sometimes…
because what you say you can't take back."
—SANDY

15

LAND OF WANDERING

"What the hell was that!" Cain shouted.

"What's what?" Lissa hissed as she squeezed my hand once more before letting go. "You're gonna have to be a little more specific, asshole."

"You know exactly what I'm talking about." Cain crossed his arms over his chest. "Jude just told me you're the reason my girlfriend just danced like—" He stammered as his eyes finally fastened to my silent frame.

I released a breath I hadn't known I was holding. I wasn't invisible.

"Like *what*, Cain?" Lissa snapped back. She stood in her high heels and cocked her hip in a defensive stance. "A burlesque dancer, like the rest of us? So it was okay when I did it, but now you got a problem 'cause it's her?"

Laughing, Lissa turned her back to Cain as though she wasn't hurt. I knew better. I could feel it, as clearly as I saw her rosy aura encased in a dusky gray sheath. She bent over and pulled free a silky, shimmering fabric from the sack beside her dresser.

I gasped as she rose, turned, and placed my cloak back in my hands, her eyes shining with the only remaining evidence left of her tears.

She'd had my cloak hidden away all this time?

I knew it wouldn't work for humans, so Lissa could not have discovered my secret. Could she?

Cain watched our exchange and shifted nervously on his feet. "Lissa, you don't get to talk to me about my relationships, not now, not ever. Fact is, I didn't want Rona around you. She made the choice to reach out to you because she's a good person. If it were up to me, you'd never get to ruin anyone else's life ever again."

Lissa's voice shook with the faintest tremor as she replied, "I'd be really upset if I cared, but I don't, Cain. I broke up with you, remember? Maybe I just want to make sure *she* doesn't get hurt."

Cain laughed. "Really? Judging from what I saw the other night, you're right back to the same bad habits."

"Shut up! You don't know what it's like for me, Cain. You never understood. If you did, you'd be thanking me for getting your mail-order girlfriend a job."

Cain threw up his hands. "Did you even ask Rona what she wants?" His mouth twisted into a hard, unpleasant expression when Lissa didn't answer. "That's what I thought."

Nodding to himself, Cain brushed past Lissa and reached for me. "Come on, baby. Let's go home. We're done here."

With Cain here, hand outstretched, I could feel his pull on me.

Seid had also been like an enthralling and unavoidable snare.

My fingers were still tangled in the bunched cloak in my lap. I held onto it like a lifeline and tried to discern the voice of reason past my emotions.

No matter what my heart wanted, it was obvious to me now, Cain and Lissa were very much aware of one another still. Their connection hummed with life before me, a living, golden cord binding them together. The same cord that had called to me across a city. And how different my feelings might have been, had Cain not looked like Seid, had he never seen me to begin with. It would have been another mission, another failed attempt at rescuing true love.

The look in Cain's eyes shifted the longer I hesitated until I could sense his uncertainty.

I slowly stood. On the heels Mrs. Nguyen bartered for me, I was almost eye level with Cain. If I was given the chance to do this over again, would I still have chosen to know him?

I closed my eyes and placed my hand in his.

We left the dressing room behind and slipped through an abandoned office for what Cain called a "side exit." No sooner had we entered the dusty office than Cain's hands lifted my hips and my back hit the wall beside the door. I gasped as he filled the space left between us, with his solid frame keeping me aloft with his hips. My legs wrapped naturally around him as his lips drew mine in a merciless dance.

I should push him away. I should run back into the club and hide until Cain asked Lissa for help searching for me. A dozen scenarios flashed through my mind of ways I could force the two of them together. But I didn't.

His hand grazed the swell of my breast as he trailed kisses past my neck. Caged by his heat and lingering passion, his forehead pressed to mine, I realized this was all that mattered. I had nothing more than a first name and nothing to claim for myself. The only real things I had left in this life were Cain and a two-thousand-year-old cloak.

"I'm sorry I got angry back there. I love watching you dance, you know that." Cain's hands cupped my backside and lifted so I was tucked firmly against him. "But those people look at you and they see sex. And it was killing me because—because I…"

I slanted my mouth against his then pulled back with a half-hearted smile. "I love you," I whispered, afraid to speak any louder, lest the gods hear. "I may never have the chance to tell you again, so never doubt that I—"

A strangled groan escaped Cain's chest as we crashed against the wall again. His kiss grew desperate, even though he was smiling. Never had I experienced such euphoria because of another human's joy. It was infectious, this perfect rightness of being, of belonging in one moment in time.

When I placed my feet on the ground, Cain only tightened his hold on me, burying his face in my neck and breathing deeply in. He murmured things against my skin, and the flush of his breath sent shivers down my spine.

Tell him. Tell that you can't stay with him, before you break him completely, my inner callous and immortal self demanded. But I couldn't, at least not now and especially after snippets of his senseless murmuring met my ears.

"—love you, until my last breath, forever."

I believe I expected for it to end then. Surely Seid would intervene, and I would open my eyes to another location, another mission. I had broken all the rules. My whispered declaration was unforgivable, even though this was an ending, rather than the beginning my traitorous heart longed for. The only beginning Cain and I could have was the promise of eternal farewell. We were using borrowed time either way, I realized.

Time that belongs to her.

We walked back to Cain's apartment instead of "hailing a cab," as we had on the way over. His spirits were so high I couldn't help but laugh at his childishness. Every time a snowflake came fluttering down from the skies, he tilted his head back to try and catch it with his tongue. When the wind continued to thwart his efforts, he made me attempt it.

I never missed.

"Not fair when you use your superpowers, Wonder Woman," he said.

My feet ached but I cared little, because his smile never left his face. To see someone so burdened by life exude so much joy because of me was thrilling.

I shivered at the unwelcome memory of Lissa as she told

me about their child.

"I want to know everything about you, Rona." Cain secured his arm around my shoulders and added, "I want to know more about where you come from and how you ended up in this part of the city, of all places. You may think it's got to be some big secret, but you can tell me."

"I do not think you will like this tale. I have never been good with words," I confessed.

Cain shrugged and sidestepped, bringing me with him, to avoid the grating in the sidewalk releasing a constant pulse of billowing steam. "No worries. You know I'm no poet, right?"

"Poet?" I wrinkled my nose at the idea. We'd had many poets in my time, people who heralded the public from the streets.

"Course, you'd never know. I could be the heir to the Dr. Seuss fortune." The mirth in his eyes stole his gravity. Obviously he was teasing me, and I had no knowledge of this doctor he spoke of.

"If you were rich, you would not be working as a bodyguard at the club," I said with a grin.

Cain cracked his knuckles and raised a dark eyebrow. "I can see I'm going to have to prove it to you, then. How about we make an even trade? You show me what it's like to be you, and when we get home, I'll show you what I can do." A smile broke through his bravado, his gaze conveying an entirely new meaning to his promise.

With a start, I realized our roles had somehow been reversed. Now I was the powerful immortal and Cain, the love-struck human. Once, I had proposed a similar question to a god.

"What it is like to be you, my love?"

Seid tipped my chin to look at him. "I am the storm, and the rain, and the winds that carry them in. It happens because I exist, because I was created to make it happen."

"Rona?" Cain tipped my chin in a familiar gesture that sent shivers down my spine.

"I do not know if it will work," I blurted to the man who so eerily resembled my first love.

"We won't know till you try, right? Come on, it'll be fun." Taking my hand in his, Cain led us to the mouth of an empty alleyway. After checking all possible outlets to the street with precision, he returned his focus to me. Releasing me, he then crossed his arms and smirked. "Okay, impress me."

"I do not know what you want me to do," I answered with a sigh and scowl at my palms.

His grin nearly split his face in two. "Besides staying with me forever, I can think of a few things," he said.

I shook my head and clenched then relaxed my palms. I paced the short width of the alley and glanced up at the gray skies. Finally, I shut my eyes and opened myself to the gifts that had come with Seid's punishment.

Colors slowly pulled from the shadowed world around us into my body, until my body grew light, insubstantial from our gritty surroundings. I was different this time, less like a wraith and more godlike than I'd felt before.

I opened my eyes to a kaleidoscope of colors emanating from my arms, casting light over the alley and Cain. His aura shone a bright happy blue against the falling flakes of ice.

Smiling, I called on the clouds above to fall more heavily, to rain thicker. Within seconds, flurries of snow fell between us.

Cain brushed my cheek with the pad of his thumb, wonder in his eyes. "So is this skill number two? You know, besides the tie-dye in your skin?"

"Does this not impress you?" I said, thinking of the impossible feats I had done over time in the name of love. "I could call on lightning to strike you dead," I suggested. "I could ask the winds to blow so fast they break through glass."

I advanced until Cain's back pressed against the gritty brick wall. The heat of our breath came together as one cloud as I added, "I can do anything I must, to rescue true love."

Cain's arms wrapped loosely around me until our bodies were pressed together and my bare legs no longer felt the cold. "Why true love?"

"Because the man who killed my husband was not a man at all," I began. "He was something more, yet my love made him less than he had been. His powers were weaker when he was with me, not as unsteady as they needed to be…"

Telling the tale while looking into the mirror image of Seid nearly made me flinch. Cain's fingers tightened their hold against my back, and I drew courage from his touch.

"Seid was the storm, and the winds, and the sea. I was his light beacon, keeping him away from the rocks. But in the end, he thought I betrayed him." I choked on my words, for this was the first time I relived the moment with remorse instead of anger.

Cain brushed snow from my hair and shoulders then caressed the line of my jaw. "I think I get it now," he said. "He was wrong, obviously, but he made you like this so, in a way, you'd never leave him."

I nodded, troubled by the too-similar tilt of his mouth and the knowing in his eyes. When he tipped my chin to meet his gaze, my memories fell silent, and there was only us.

Brushing his lips against mine, he whispered low, "What I don't get is how you could fall in love with anyone after what he put you through. How long have you been like this?"

I hesitated, only because I was afraid this might make him want me less. His lifespan, after all, was like a blink of my eye. "More than two of your millennia."

His reaction was not what I expected.

"Damn!" Cain shook his head and laughed. "Wow, that makes you the grandma of all cougars, doesn't it?"

"What is a cougar?" I asked.

Cain lifted me into his arms and laughed.

"His...ability to overcome troubles in his past."
— AMBER

16

Time Mends

Mrs. Nguyen was smoking outside her apartment with another neighbor when we arrived, snow soaked and exhausted. Cain carried me in his arms, yet somehow we managed to unlock the door. I used my feet to kick it inside, sharing a secret smile with Mrs. Nguyen from over his shoulder.

Cain was so tired he could hardly keep his eyes open, but he insisted on chasing me through his apartment. His idea of a game, he declared, was to see if he could undo Mrs. Nguyen's gift of a torture-chamber dress, he said. My modesty won for only so long, and then I let him kiss me sweetly beneath the thick blankets, entwined.

I told myself I was truly happy, but happiness, as everyone knows, is a fickle, fleeting thing.

"You accept me so easily," I said later, when the moon was at its zenith. "Any other human would not have believed me, but you do. Why?"

Cain smiled and buried his face in my unbound hair. "Because I love you, Rona. I already told you I was crazy. If love makes normal people do crazy things, you can't even begin to imagine what I would do for you. Plus, it's kind of hard to ignore rainbow skin."

My answering grin was tempered by the way the curse had backfired on Cain the other night. Why had it chosen to punish us then for breaking the rules but not now? Was it possible *I* had possessed the ability to control the curse all along?

"You mentioned you had done terrible things." I traced the scars on Cain's chest and the one that marred his face. "What is it you did that haunts you so?"

Cain's expression flattened as memories clouded his stormy gaze. When he finally began, his voice was barely a rasping whisper. "The government shipped me up here, to my uncle and aunt's. Wasn't long before I got mixed up in the wrong crowd. My aunt was so afraid I'd end up with a bullet in my head one day that she practically begged me to join the army, like it was a better alternative. Which was cool and all, I thought. A lot of guys were just as gung-ho to serve after what happened with the towers. My dad had been in the marines and Gramps was in World War Two… so it just seemed natural, like it was my turn, you know?"

I laced our fingers together during his pause and traced his swollen knuckles.

"When I joined up, I was just another grunt. I loved everything about my job until the war." He shut his eyes, mouth working past the flux of bad memories. "Then, our unit got trapped in the city. We were cut off from reinforcements and told to hold out. We spent months living off the streets, taking whatever we had to after our rations ran out. I got slashed in the face by a scared kid trying to defend his home when we came looting for food… When I came back, everything was just different. I had a hard time fitting in with the world after what I'd done. It was too easy to fall back in with my old crowd. They were older, and I came back, and well, for a while, I became the guy who made others keep their promises, if you know what I mean. If they didn't pay up, I left them reminders as to why they should."

Wrapping my hands around his clenched fists, I interrupted, "But you chose a different path again."

His eyes studied me intently for a long moment before his lips tilted up at the corner. "It was my aunt's doing. She died of lung cancer about a year ago, but not before I made a promise to her to try again. I never made it to college, but my uncle pulled some strings with an old war buddy of his, a foreman for one of the big corporations. Guy taught me the ropes, and I took some courses, bought some tools, and there you go."

"And have you fulfilled your aunt's promise then?" Cain's look pierced me, another reminder he did not truly belong to me.

"Almost. She made me promise I'd start playing again before she died, but I just haven't had the heart to pick it up again. Maybe now…" He trailed off with a yawn before tucking me in closer beneath his chin.

I held onto him and watched as color played off my skin in the darkness like colored starlight. So much pain we had both endured. Wasn't it enough?

Cain had seen through the curse. If it had truly broken, and I was gifted with a human life, would I be allowed to keep Cain? And if not, where could I go? My home sank into the sea with an earthquake ages ago. Even if I somehow found my distant relatives, they would only make me homesick for the ones I'd lost.

Yet should I choose to finish what I had set out to do, if I brought Cain and Lissa back together, Cain's memory of me would evaporate like sun-drenched dew.

Drawing my courage to speak, I lifted my head only to find Cain fast asleep. I sighed as I settled onto the steady rise and fall of his chest. Tomorrow I needed to tell Cain the whole truth and hold nothing back. I must confront him about Lissa and insist that, if nothing else, he needed to forgive her.

Cain nuzzled his lips against the crown of my forehead in his sleep. Clenching my eyelids shut, I fought the thrill racing through my skin and brushed the traitorous tears away.

I trembled when I saw the look in my new husband's eyes. I dug my nails into my palms to push my fears back as his fingers pressed bruises into my shoulders. His breath was hot and foul as he spoke, "Did you think me a fool, Orona? Your father learned of it first. But I was too taken in by your beauty to believe him."

"I—" My words were stunted by the impact of his hand against my face, and cold fire tingled beneath my cheek.

"Do not speak. Do not breathe another word of your treachery, witch." His laugh was warm and too rich, too pleasant to belong to such a monster.

"Husband!" I began, hoping to plead to that spark I once

saw in his eye, repulsive as it might have been to me.

"Did you think I would not follow you? After everything I did to acquire you, the money I gave your father just to shut him up, did you not think I would care? That I would not see the creature my wife was cavorting with?"

I cried out in pain when he ripped my dress from my body, but he did not stop. His touches were brutal, forcing me to remember whom I belonged to. Tears fell in steady streams down my cheeks, but I refused to cry out again. So it became my husband's mission to see, to make me scream.

"SEID!" I begged for my love, not to come for me but to step no further. My god had come at last and in the worst possible moment.

I wanted to cover my face in shame. I had promised I wouldn't betray him to keep my family's honor, to save those who had sold me to this man. I had promised I would run away to Seid and never look back. He had vowed to look after my family from afar, claimed they would want for nothing.

I had broken my promise.

Poseidon appeared from the air itself, carried through the terrace by an unnatural wind. My god's flesh swirled so dark a blue, like the eye of a storm. Thunder cracked when he spoke, and lightning flashed in patterns just beneath the layer of his skin.

My husband was ripped from me by Seid's powerful hand. I cried from relief as he held the monster aloft and drowned my husband slowly from the inside out. I couldn't discern Seid's words through the crack and rumble bringing *the rains overhead. I welcomed them, wanted to wash them away.*

After he was finished, Seid looked at me, and I was terrified by what I saw in his cold gaze.

Snatching me up, Seid drew me to his chest until we became one with the rains and the clouds. We flew on the wind, and the sensation of being so light was as beautiful as the first time. Only now I felt true fear, a fear that struck me deeper than the thought of losing my life to my husband.

I had broken my promise to a god.

"Seid!" I reached for him, but his image blurred and dissipated like smoke. When I opened my eyes, I was sitting up in Cain's bed. Panting, I was brought back down to the pillows by Cain's firm but gentle grasp. Those hands continued to brush along my heated skin, pushing wet hair off my cheeks and forehead.

I ran an absent hand over my thighs, where my husband's whip lashes should have been. But the scars had long ago healed over. Reluctantly, I met Cain's gaze and knew the sun would soon rise above the veil of clouds.

"You've said his name in your sleep before," he said. "Was Seid the bastard who made you like this?"

I nodded. "Once, I was forced to marry the wealthiest man my father knew. He bought me for my beauty."

"You were married," Cain echoed. "But not to Seid?"

I shook my head. "Seid was the one who rescued me before my husband could kill me."

Cain released a long breath and frowned at the ceiling. A

pained detachment entered his voice when next he spoke. "So what was this guy? You already knew him, and that's why he rescued you, I'm assuming. But why would he save and then curse you the next minute?"

I dragged my finger along Cain's scars and wished I could soak up his pain, past and present. "Seid was—It was like he was made from the storm and sea itself. His nature was violent and unstable. But I made him too stable, distracted."

I closed my eyes and pressed my cheek to Cain's arm as I continued, "He killed my husband for beating me, but he wanted to punish me for breaking my promise."

"What? That's some first-class bullshit, Rona," Cain growled.

"You do not break promises to gods, Cain," I whispered. "They are not driven by their natures, and do not reason like humans. Seid thought I chose to leave him, after promising I would run away with him. He didn't understand what it was to be bound by family duty and honor…" I trailed off, unable to go any further. Bile rose in the back of my throat as I relived the times my husband whipped me into submission. I was so lost to the past and that final dark hour, that I didn't recognize my point of view had changed. Was I truly defending Seid?

I pulled away from Cain as I added, "I should not be telling you any of this. I should not have shared your bed… I should return to the magical couch."

He snatched my wrist and tugged until he could gather me in the safety of his arms. "Please don't go. Stay. You keep the nightmares away. Not even she did that."

"You mean Lissa?" I softly intoned and shivered when he

sighed heavily against my neck.

"You don't still think you're supposed to get us back together, do you? Not after what you admitted last night." He pressed a kiss to my temple.

I closed my eyes and told him the painful truth. "What I said does not change what I was brought here to do."

I could feel Cain's rising panic almost instantly through my connection to him. This was one of the greatest differences between the mortal and immortal men I had loved. Seid had always been so assured and confident, until the day he cursed me.

"Rona, you've got to be—"

"You have to at least try, Cain. I will not be responsible for ruining your last chance for joy in this life."

"Baby, *you* are the only thing that makes me happy," he crooned against my ear, trying to turn me around to face him. But I refused, knowing I could not hold my resolve while looking into that familiar face.

"You say so now," I replied, "but how can you know for certain? You need to try, Cain, for all of our sakes. Try to remember what it was like when she made your sun rise and set every day."

"Yeah, sure, look past all the ways she used and abandoned me," Cain said with a bitter laugh. "You of all people should know how hard that is, Rona. Can you honestly tell me you still feel the same about Seid?"

I shook my head, unwilling to go there when the answer would make me face things I was not ready for. "What you and I have is a new love, Cain. But what Seid and I shared—what you and Lissa share—*this* is true. I do not know why you are able to see me or why you dream of the sea…"

I hesitated and came so dangerously close to telling Cain the awful truth, that I was first drawn to him because he looked like Seid. Instead, I pushed aside the mad impulse and said, "I have no right to make you love me, or to love you. But I do know that love is something that is tested and mended over time."

Cain pressed his lips to the crux of my neck and shoulder. "You realize this talk is only making me love you more?"

"I wish you loved me a little less," I confessed.

Cain crawled so he was half on top of me and supported his weight on his elbow. He used his free hand to draw patterns over my skin. "If this is you trying to make me fall out of love with you, it's not working."

"You are trying to change the subject," I replied, frustrated with my body's reaction to his touch as much as his inability to take this seriously.

"Well, I learned from the best," he said and then kissed me until his morning alarm brought us both back to reality.

After I helped Cain dress for his day job and prepare a quick meal, he grudgingly promised he would try.

"You must learn to forgive her if you wish to truly heal from your past," I said.

Cain simply smirked. "Can't fix something that's already broken, but I'll try for you."

As I watched Cain leave through the open doorway, I wondered if he was right, if I could stay here forever.

Be human. Learn to live again.

For the second time in the six days I had known Cain, I allowed myself to believe.

And once more, a sharp stab of pain jabbed beneath my healed scars. This pain intensified until it was amplified fifty times fifty over.

I collapsed before the threshold in a silent scream as the curse forced my flesh to burn with an invisible fire.

"I don't think anyone knows the definition of love until they are truly sure
they've found it, and if they do find it, how can they be so sure?"
—ANONYMOUS

17

Understanding Lissa

"Snap out of it, sugar! Come on! That's a good girl. Breathe." Smoke-tainted breath washed over my face, accompanied by the faint scent of lilac and cloves that permeated Mrs. Nguyen's skin. I roused to find her black eyes shining and her red-painted lips turning up into a full smile. "See, I knew you wouldn't run off and leave Mrs. Nguyen."

I leaned into the warmth her small body gave me. Somehow she had managed to shut the door, drag me over to the couch, and wrap me in Cain's mother's shawl in the moments following my blackout.

"How did you—what did you see?" My voice fell flat when I glanced down and saw my skin was still a brightly mottled mosaic of colors. Gasping, I met her knowing gaze and frowned. Realization dawned in the aftermath of my fear. "You knew?"

She picked up the cigarette she had earlier discarded on a nearby table and inhaled deeply before answering. "I always believed aliens existed, just never expected you to be prettier than us."

I was prepared to disagree, until I saw the teasing glint in her black eye. I was certain then she would not expose my secret. I fell back with a groan. "Any other human would have run away screaming or forgotten about me."

"Kind of hard to forget seeing a girl with rainbow skin, huh?" Mrs. Nguyen chuckled deeply in her chest and ignored her rattling cough that accompanied it. "Ducky, I don't care what color skin you have, long as you don't break our boy's heart."

I relaxed into her lap and smiled as Mrs. Nguyen ran her fingers through my tangled curls. My mother had never been so kind or understanding. She had heard my sister's whispers and was the first to inflict punishment on me for my disobedience. This was how I first learned women were capable of cruelty just like men. Internal scars are not so quick to heal.

Thinking of Seid's curse and the warning I had been given, I confessed, "I fear Cain only loves me because he still grieves for Lissa and all they have lost."

I didn't know how much Mrs. Nguyen knew of Cain and Lissa's relationship. Not even Cain realized how much I knew of their past.

"Ah, I see. You think he's sad because of the baby." She tapped her nose and smiled. "I may be a crazy old lady from Brooklyn, but I know a lot more of what goes around here than people think."

"So you know he still loves her?"

After exhaling a fresh wreath of smoke over our heads, Mrs. Nguyen answered, "I think you're obsessing so much over what love is or isn't, you're missing the big picture."

"What do you mean?"

"I mean you need to get out there. Go talk to Lissa. You can't make this thing happen, sugar. Love ain't all magic and fairy tales. Sometimes, you just hope you find someone who can put up with you long enough to commit." Forcing me to sit up, she handed me her smoke and said, "Now, take a drag of that and come get some of my special tea. Let's see about what clothes you'll need to stop that boy's heart."

"But I should not be trying to draw his attention. I should be—"

"Shut up and let me have my fun," Mrs. Nguyen interrupted.

When I arrived at the club later, trusting the note Mrs. Nguyen wrote Cain and left in his apartment, I found it to be the center of activity. People walked in and around the building and spoke with men and women dressed in black-and-yellow uniforms.

I had used my gift and my cloak to arrive undetected, but now I had no clue how to avoid drawing more on the curse. Once I tapped into the source inside of me, it was nearly impossible to stop. I would be forced to become transparent again, just to avoid bumping into people.

After weaving through the crowd, I turned at the familiar voice arguing with the throng of women around him. "Look, Ginger, how many times I gotta tell you, smoke your joints *outside* the club! Not right underneath a damn smoke detector!"

It was the redhead I had seen the night before, the one who kept her things on the dresser beside Lissa's. Ginger didn't hesitate to challenge her employer's authority in front of the other girls. "Yo, I only took like two puffs! No reason to call the DEA on this place."

I cautiously edged through the space between them, not daring to breathe.

Jude ran a hand over his face and groaned. When he spoke I could smell the coffee and faint taint of alcohol on his breath. "Those weren't the DEA, *doll*, and if you'd gone to high school, you'd know the difference between feds and the fire department."

Cocking her hip, Ginger glanced back at the other girls. "I got the best education I'll ever need on these streets. Matter of fact, I got to know some cops and a teacher or two better outside the classroom."

Another girl, a brunette, laughed. "Can you remember that far back, Ginger?"

Another squabble quickly began. Jude hung his head in his hands.

I cringed, sympathizing with his frustration. My sisters had been equally difficult to tether. I was almost to the club door when one of the dancers called out, "Hey! What's with the chick under the trench?"

"What if she's DEA?" another exclaimed. Cursing, they began to worry over their possessions.

Jude's voice cut over their chatter. "For the love of the gods, it's just Cain's new girl. Hey, new girl, your man ain't here!"

I tightened my grip on the cloak that should have been firmly in place and glanced down at the threadbare fabric.

Has it ceased working completely? Was the curse's attack more than a warning?

"Orona? What are you doing out here, chica! And dressed like this when it's freezing." Lissa appeared out of nowhere, throwing her own cigarette to the ground before clasping my hand in hers and pulling me around the back.

"Where are we going?" I asked. I glanced over my shoulder to find Jude's curious gaze trained on us while he spoke with one of the uniformed men.

"Ginger tripped the smoke alarm...stupid stoner. I'm hiding out up in the loft 'till the smoke clears. Jude would flip if he knew I was taking you up here. But he's the one who called you Cain's new girl," she said with a shrug.

Lissa's mahogany curls bounced in front of me, nearly half as long as her curvy figure. Without those stick-like heels on her feet, she was at least a head shorter than me. Her heavy jacket, baggy pants, and boots were also the complete opposite of her usual glamorous attire.

She led me up a rickety metal stair braced into the side of the building. Once again, I saw remnants of a time gone by in the dated style of the brick apartments and businesses. At one time, this part of their city was considered beautiful. At the head of the stairs, a heavy metal door awaited us.

Lissa released my hand to push the already cracked door aside. "Just bang it shut real hard," she called before rushing ahead of me into her temporary home. When I did as she asked, a crack formed in the wall connected to the doorframe.

Oops...

Lissa didn't notice now that she had turned a corner and stuck her face through yet another doorframe. "Hey, Pops, you awake yet?"

"Girl, don't disrespect your elders," a muffled voice answered.

"How am I disrespecting you, old man?" Lissa asked.

"You forgot to knock."

"How is that gonna make you any more of a morning person?"

While they argued, I inspected the loft Cain had described and I had glimpsed from his childhood memories. Warmth filled every orifice, betraying a lingering feminine influence. Pictures covered the walls in shades of black and white. No doubt they were tacked with a sea of famous faces, but I have never kept track with musicians and players in the theater. It was a pointless pursuit when their lives passed by me so quickly, only reminding me that I was unchangeable.

At the opposite end of the vast floor was an open bar and kitchen area. Another entryway decorated by heavy chains and locks stood next to it. This was obviously the more popular exit, since there was a rack for coats and a woven mat for catching excess dirt. Further in, the entertainment area was populated by a curious blend of old and new furniture. The giant box I once heard called "tee-vee" flashed with lifelike images of richly dressed people. As I walked on the gleaming hardwood floor, I realized how ridiculous my heeled boots appeared and paused to remove them.

"Okay! I'll bring it to ya in a sec!" Lissa called back before twisting to greet me. Pasting a strained smile on her face, she did not meet my eyes before motioning to the couch. "You can chill here while I make the old man a sandwich."

I sank into a leathery couch that was so much softer than Cain's magical bed. I smiled when I found an old radio similar to the one in his apartment. Except this one was littered in picture frames of varying sizes. The faces smiled and occasionally frowned out from the pictures trapped within. Once I refocused my sight to cross the greater distance, I could see each and every face and at last saw evidence to a life Cain happily lived.

As a boy, he stood on a sleek white ship, his arm wrapped around a younger girl with curly black hair and dark eyes. Who was the little girl? She looked so similar to him, though subtly different. Her nose was more rounded and her skin a darker shade, yet their wide grins were the same. Was this his sister? And if she was, why had he never spoken of her before?

"So, Cain must have told you the good news?"

Jumping slightly, I reached to curl my hair around my fingers and faced Lissa. "Good news?"

Lissa rolled her eyes as she applied the last of her ingredients on the sandwich she was making for Pop. "Seriously? He can't let anyone be happy, can he? What are you, like his maid or something? Are you running from the FBI and don't have nowhere else to go? Because I know a guy who could get you the papers you need, if you know what I'm saying."

I found my gaze again wandering to the little girl a younger Cain kept his arm around.

"Hey, you okay? Orona? What are you looking at?" Lissa walked around the kitchen counter until she was blocking my line of sight. Cocking her hip and balancing the sandwich plate and drink in her hands, she said, "Chica, you may dance better than any of Jude's little hoes, but if you're gonna work for him, you need to start learning some social skills."

"Lissa?" the elderly voice called. "Who you talking to out there, girl? Where's my three-course meal?"

Pausing in her study of me, Lissa stomped over to the bedroom. "Nobody, Pops. She's just a friend of mine who just started working downstairs, okay?"

I crossed the room until I stood before the picture-laden stereo. Only one other picture showed the little girl, perhaps a year or two later. Her brightly smiling face was unaltered, but Cain's had faded about the edges. His arms were wrapped completely around her thin frame this time, drawing her more tightly to him than in the previous photo. The girl's hair had been replaced by a colorful scarf.

"That's Amy," Lissa said, suddenly at my side. It was the softest tone I had ever heard her use before. "Cain never talks about her, and I never really met her when we went to high school. Jude told me she died of leukemia when she was seven."

"She was his sister." I clutched my cloak with one hand and brushed aside tears with the other.

Lissa watched me curiously. Though she could never understand the tragedy of living after everyone she had ever loved was gone, I wanted to tell her anyway. The memory resurfaced of the day I returned to my island, only to find my parents dead and my surviving sisters wrinkled and white haired.

Time was not a kind friend to an immortal.

"Cain hasn't told you about her yet, I take it?" Lissa inquired.

I couldn't help but stare at the pictures of Amy and wondered what kind of terror she had suffered, knowing she would die so young.

"You know, Jude once told me that's how he'd know if Cain found the one," Lissa said. "He'd be able to tell her everything, about how his alcoholic dad killed himself and his mama by capsizing in a storm. Or how Cain thought it was his fault for not pouring out the booze before they got on the boat that night."

She paused to lean against the stereo, eyeing me. "I wouldn't worry about it. He didn't tell me, and I still broke his heart." Lissa shrugged and slapped her hands on the dusty wood, leaving oily traces of her prints behind.

She sank back onto the couch and picked up a black-button-covered stick. "You wanna watch some cartoons? I gotta have at least a solid hour of Cartoon Network before I'm ready to entertain," she said without waiting to see if I agreed.

I sat down next to Lissa and was amazed by her ability to deflect emotions. Through our connection and her aura, I knew she felt everything deeply. After watching her stare numbly at the "tee-vee," I attempted to drive her into conversation. "You didn't go home with Derek last night?"

Lissa's eyebrows drew together. "Who told you about Derek?"

"You mentioned him the night we went out," was my honest reply.

A flash of fear came and went in her green gaze before she focused on the screen and said, "Guess I shouldn't be surprised. I talk too much when I'm drunk. Besides, you probably would have heard it from Cain eventually."

Lissa grimaced and bent her head to play with the frayed edge of her shirt. "You know, I—I went back to Cain a couple of times after Jude. But Derek has always been into me, like *really* into me, you know? You were with Cain during the storm, right? Well, I went home with Derek that night."

Lissa trailed off and rubbed her hand over her flat belly. I thought of the bruises and the blood she had coughed into her hand in Derek's apartment. And how she had drunkenly whispered at the club where we danced, *I should have known better…but he said the pills wouldn't hurt. Oh God, what if Cain finds out?*

"Lissa…" I rested my hand just over the bruise her sleeve concealed. Lissa startled as she turned to face me. There was hope hidden behind the vulnerability in her eyes as I continued, "You must stop seeing Derek. This man does not love you, I fear. And nothing you do can convince him to love you."

Lissa jerked away from my touch. "Not that it's any of *your* business, but I didn't go home with Derek last night. Besides, he'll be back from his business trip tonight. And if he asks, I'm going with him."

"Lissa, please don't do this," I begged. "When you experience the kind of love you and Cain shared, you do not simply toss it aside. Remember this before you throw your lot in with a man who cannot love you."

"Where do you get off!" Lissa jumped to her feet. "It's like you want to get me and Cain back together! Why the hell would you want that? You talk about not throwing away a man like him, but isn't that what *you're* doing? Don't you know what an amazing guy he is?"

I stood and reached for her hands but she batted me aside. "Lissa, I know you are afraid, but running away won't solve anything. Wealth will not provide you the happiness or security you imagine. People, and the love they give, is what melds us together."

Lissa threw her hands up, unwilling to hear anymore. "Sorry, Rona, but I'm not getting into this again with you."

"If you would only try—"

Lissa stamped her heel to the ground. "It's too late! Don't you get that? I had a good thing, and I threw it away. You think I don't know this already?"

I clasped my hands before my chest and *willed* her to listen. "You could have gone to Cain with your fears, and he would have understood. Why did you not give him a chance to take care of you, instead of running to a man you barely knew?"

Lissa stumbled back a step and glared up at me with splotches of red on her face. "Derek had the means to help me get rid of the baby. It was what *I* wanted, Rona. I'm not gonna make it if I end up like my ma, with six kids and a shitty roach-infested apartment!"

"What's going on out there, Lissa?" Pops called from the other room. "You okay, honey?"

"Nothing, Pop! Cain's friend was just leaving." She pulled her lips back in the tightest of smiles. "I think it's safe to go downstairs now. You should talk to Jude about what he wants you to perform tonight."

I followed Lissa to the door that would lead me down to the club. Yet instead of going through the opening she held open for me, I turned to Lissa and said, "Forgive me for causing you pain. I know you think me strange for believing this, but I want you to be happy, Lissa. And you and Cain will never find joy until you can forgive one another first."

"…our vow to…work through our issues together."
—LAURA

18

Human Understanding

The door slammed shut behind me. The narrow stairwell I descended eventually opened to a dark hole that seemed ready to swallow me whole.

As I followed the pull of music below, the memory ascended so heavily I could taste tears on my tongue.

Seid dropped me onto the sandbar, our favorite place. The waves crashed around us, though they never touched the sphere of his influence.

Trying to gather my dignity, I gathered what remained of my tattered dress to cover my chest.

Seid's eyes brewed with malice and fury as he approached. Our eyes never broke contact as he delicately snapped the remaining ties of the soiled fabric and threw it into the sea.

I watched in awe as he gathered seafoam and shells and then summoned dark clouds for the lightning he needed to weave his creation together. What he crafted for me was of a silvery blue fabric so lovely I could almost forget the hard look in his eye as he placed the cloak in my hands and stepped back.

"Seid?" I whispered, trembling still from our close call.

A muscle popped in his jaw, and he took another step back.

"Seid?" When I tried to follow him, to wrap my arms around him, I tripped and fell to my knees. Seid didn't move to help me up, and true fear lifted the hairs at my neck.

Never break a promise to a god.

"It wasn't their fault!" I pleaded, recognizing the sneer in his perfect lips. He blamed my father for what had happened, I knew. My god's wrath when angered was legendary, and when sparked, few could escape his fury.

"No more!" he growled, lifting a finger to me.

The changes began immediately. Gills broke my skin apart in tiny bloody slivers underneath his invisible touch. He had done this before to show me his home beneath the waves. Yet this time was different. This time other parts of me began to change and twist into something lighter, dangerous and powerful.

"What are you doing to me?" I rasped, clutching my chest where the pain began to concentrate and grow. "My love, please!"

Thunder rolled over our heads as he spoke. "You betrayed me."

The pain was unbearable as Seid inflicted his wrath on me with the force of his will. Those glorious blue eyes were frozen into cold and dark seas, indifferent to my screams. In all our tumultuous and tender times together, I had never believed he would use his power on me.

"I pledged myself to you!" I cried. "Why are you doing this?"

"You know why," he seethed.

"But I didn't truly betray you! You would have known if I had! Please, it is not their fault, Seid. Spare them, and punish me!"

My pain ceased, and a cruel smile transformed his features into something dangerously beautiful.

"Will you avow yourself to my will?"

"Anything."

The past blurred into the present, and I realized I had fallen into the stairs some time ago. I clutched the railing with my hands to hang onto something as I was forced to relive my past.

The curse crashed through my body just as passionately as it had the first time. A ripping and mending of flesh took place in aftershocks, in the memory of true pain. For the second time in a day's span, Seid's curse reminded me not only who but *what* I was. And in my mind, I felt the sting of betrayal afresh.

This most recent warning felt more personal and frightening. I had broken the rules, and my secret fear was fading away before I could see Cain one last time. I never believed in a happy ending for myself, not since Seid cursed me. But knowing Cain had taught me to hope as I hadn't allowed myself in two thousand years. The idea of losing this awareness, the gift of feeling again, scared me.

I was so overcome that I didn't hear his approach and

flinched at the sound of his voice. "Hey, you okay, sugar? Looks like you could use a drink," Jude said at the foot of the stairs, his silhouette covering me.

I stared numbly up at Cain's cousin, not quite hearing his words, until he reached his hand out to me and smiled. "Come on. I don't bite...much."

ᔕᔕᔕ

Two glassfuls of amber liquid later left us in the same place we had started. My miniature glasses remained untouched before me, yet Jude continued to pour. I could see that he was hoping the liquor might convince me to open up to working for him.

"So how long have you known my cousin? It can't have been too long, even if he managed to somehow hide you in that rats' nest of his."

I frowned at Jude's unpleasant choice of words, yet the moment I thought of Cain's home, I answered, "It feels like forever."

Jude swirled the drink in his glass and observed me. "I think I believe you. But I'd feel a lot better if I knew you were a citizen before hiring you. That accent of yours is something else. What part of the world are you from, honey?"

I was curious as to why he would compare me to food, but answered truthfully. "My home is little more than a ruin. I will not go back."

"Okay, guess that answers that question..." Jude laughed. "You do realize this is a kind of informal interview, don't you?"

"Cain does not wish for me to perform for you."

Jude chuckled with the confidence of a man used to getting his way. I still hadn't decided if this made him more or less appealing. "Oh, you wouldn't only be dancing for me, not that I wouldn't enjoy it."

Jude spread his hands in an open gesture. "I guess I've been going about this the wrong way. English is obviously your second language. So tell me, honey. What's it gonna take to get you back on that stage?"

"Not unless you can convince Cain to play again." I crossed my arms over my chest. While outwardly I tried to maintain a stoic calm, inside my heart was racing. Jude was still Cain's employer and might not appreciate me giving ultimatums.

But Cain promised his aunt. This could help to heal some of his grief.

Jude stared at me a moment longer then laughed. "Cain? Are you seriously telling me he wants to play again, after ten years? Mr. Happy wants to moonlight as a musician."

"I think you should let him play his instrument," I simply stated, angered by his doubt. The answer seemed so obvious I wondered that he hadn't seen it. Cain loved music. This is why he chose to work here.

And maybe it's the key to fulfilling your mission.

Jude fought a grin before saying, "So you think you've figured my baby cuz out already? After spending a week holed up in that flat of his, well, that's impressive."

I frowned, not appreciating his tone yet not fully comprehending his meaning. "I sense you say things you do not mean. But I speak the truth."

Jude observed me from over the rim of his glass before

leaning over the bar and saying, "I like you, blondie. Tell you what. You manage to convince my little cousin to get on that stage, and I'll make sure he has a spot tomorrow night. We got a deal?"

I was still unused to acting spontaneously. Without emotion, my sense of what I needed to do had seemed so simple. Yet I knew, once the words left my mouth, Cain needed to start playing as much as Lissa needed to stay away from Derek. So I accepted Jude's proffered hand and returned his smile. "The bargain is struck."

"Yo, boss!" A thin, chocolate-skinned girl tossed up a hand as she walked past us and slowed once her eyes fell on me. I, too, froze as I began to recognize the girl who guarded the club patrons' cloaks from that first night.

Jude grumbled something under his breath while tossing down the last of his drink. "Chloe, how many times have I told you not to be late? What do you think I'm paying you for?"

The girl sniffed and smoothed her beautifully styled hair. "You and me both know I've got the best assets of any of your girls," she said with a wink. Looking at me, Chloe waved. "Good luck, new girl. Great moves, by the way."

Jude shook his head as Chloe darted off to the dressing rooms and poured himself another glass.

"You drink too much," I observed.

He paused, eyes widening a fraction of a hair. "Now I'm starting to see why my little cousin keeps you around. You're a comedienne and an exotic dancer, best of both worlds, honey."

Lissa appeared behind Jude from the apartment stair and leaned onto his shoulder. "Pop's been asking for you." She flinched when her gaze drifted and met mine.

Jude's relaxed demeanor shifted, and his hand on Lissa's back was gentle, affectionate even. "Keep an eye on things down here for me, will you, babe?"

I slipped off the stool and donned my cloak once more as Lissa nodded her agreement. They didn't even notice I was gone as they leaned closer to whisper to each other. I smiled as I watched their erratic and electric red connection fizz and dart between them. Humans had such difficulty seeing what was before their own eyes.

As I melded into the background, I wished things could be so simple for all of us. How easy it would be to remain human forever, for the curse to break and all of us find our individual happiness. After my failed attempt to get through to Lissa, and my struggle against my curse, I wasn't sure I should hope for the impossible anymore.

"We…enjoy each other's company even when we have nothing
to say to each other…" —ANONYMOUS

19

Cain did not work at the club that night. Instead he cooked dinner and turned on his stereo before we shared his attempt at what he called a Korean dish. After dinner, we danced to the music, a tangle of hands and caresses.

An hour later, Cain left to check on Mrs. Nguyen and bring her the leftovers of our meal.

And to learn her opinion, I imagined.

Exchanging the simplicity of feeling for thought was not a pleasant experience, especially when my thoughts tended to remind me of the truth I'd rather ignore.

My advice to Lissa still rang in my ears. Only now I saw how it applied to my situation as well as hers. I glanced at the stereo and thought of the pictures of his sister Amy, of the older man who lived with Jude and Lissa. What else did I not know of Cain's past?

I stretched out my hands to catch the tiny clusters of ice

falling from the smoky purple sky. The window had not been difficult to open, though I might have accidently cracked some of the glass in my efforts. I smiled as snow collected in my palm. If I changed my body temperature and allowed it to merge with the gentle white storm, the ice would not melt on contact. It was beautiful, and I decided I liked the snow best of all.

What would Seid think of snow?

I sensed the moment Cain returned from Mrs. Nguyen's apartment. For a moment, I simply listened as he dug through his closet's contents, unlocked the metal clasps, and quietly began tuning his instrument. I shivered to think of those fingers trailing the skin over my neck. His fingers were rough from his work on "the site," as he called it, yet surprisingly gentle. Like now, as he effortlessly plucked music from the strings of an instrument he claimed not to have touched in years.

Sticking out my tongue, I tasted a stray snowflake and grimaced. It was not sweet as I had expected and rather tainted from the toxins floating above the city. Yet when I clenched my hand into a fist, I wondered if I could fix it.

Closing my eyes, I looked past the growing darkness inside of me until I found that soft pulsing light. When I touched it, thrills laced up and down my spine. I opened my eyes to stare at the glowing chunk of ice in my open palm, as the colors in my skin reflected through its crystalized surface. I released the trapped snow and watched it disperse into a cloud of tiny flakes again with a sigh.

If only Seid's curse had been a gift, I could have purified more than snow. Pulling away from the window, I reached up to pull the glass pane closed. Warmth instantly stole back my senses as I sat beside Cain on the couch.

He smiled at me with a light I had not seen in him before and set his instrument aside. Without a word, he seemed to sense the love pushing against the confines of my heart. I went into his arms because to not do so would have made the curse burst from its confines. And at this point, I was not sure what the full brunt of Seid's power would do to us.

Take whatever moments you have left.

Sometime after, as we watched the snow fall from the magical bed, I had the courage to ask, "Will you play your instrument at the club?"

Cain tensed behind me, frozen in fury or fear, I did not know. But I was willing to press further. I had my reasons for wanting him to play.

"I—why would you ask me that?" He choked on his words, ending with a muffled laugh against my shoulder. "Rona, I haven't played in public since I left for basic."

His voice drifted into a silence I wanted to crack. Did I dare mention everything Lissa had hinted about his mother and father and Amy?

"Would you change anything about your life, if you could?"

Cain sighed, pressing the bridge of his nose to my skin, so his breath flushed down my back. "If you'd have asked me that question a few days ago, then *yes.*"

My smile surprised me as much as the joy his words gave me. Afraid he might notice, I turned my chin to the cushion. "You cannot tell me you don't regret some of the choices you made."

My existence painted a very harsh and clear definition of regret. I knew too well the consequences of misbegotten decisions. Willing him to understand, I continued, "Didn't you ever look at your life and wish you had grasped at your chances when they were before you?"

His answer was as cold as his rigid embrace. "Living here doesn't bother me, if that's what you're saying. I don't need the finer things in life to know what counts. Are you saying you do?"

His fear tainted the air around us so thickly I could taste its sickly green aura. I turned in his arms to face him before he could compare me further to *her*.

"Cain." I traced the scar that trailed down his neck and waited until his blue eyes lifted to mine, as if he were afraid of what he might find. I felt the tension in him fade as I cupped his face with my hands and said, "I am ageless. I have no need to eat or drink, unless I want to. And being solid all of the time has been the most difficult part of my time with you…"

Slowly, he lifted his hands until they covered mine. "Rona, I know what you're trying to do."

"You do?"

"Well, you *did* tell me you were trying to hook me up with Lissa. But if you think getting me to play at the club again is going to miraculously wipe the past away, you're wrong. I can't pretend like I never met you. I know you think me and Lissa have some kind of epic love, but maybe the truth's more complicated than that."

"Cain," I said. His eyes flickered to mine, revealing the dark shadows trapped within.

Cain's fingers dragged through my hair as his words fell over my face with a warm breath. "You ever been in love before, Rona?"

"You know I have," I said, staring at him in wonder.

"And how long was it, before you knew?"

I stilled beneath his touch and remembered those horrid years immediately following Seid's curse. My immortal love had never failed to torment me, often showing up to ruin my plans or taunt me. I had fought vainly to hide my ire every time he interfered in the missions *he* gave to me. But I craved to see him as much as I hated him and hated myself all the more for wanting him still.

I could not say exactly when or why he stopped interrupting. Perhaps he finally understood after the mission when I influenced his own waters to swirl into a vortex and swallow him whole, instead of the couple I was protecting? Eventually, Seid ceased appearing altogether, and I forgot how to live outside my memories and my mission.

Cain must have seen my answer in my face because he did not hesitate to speak for me. "I know that Lissa and I have unresolved issues," he said. "It's not like we didn't already know that. We practically grew up together. She works at my family's nightclub, and I see her almost every day. She lives with my cousin and uncle, and that's part of the reason I don't make that many visits to the loft. But we've made it work so far. I know I need to forgive her, and I promised you I would."

"So play," I interrupted with a soft smile. "Nothing is stopping you."

Cain exhaled and shook his head. "You aren't letting up on this, are you?"

"Cain," I said after pressing my lips to his, "this is about *you* learning how to heal. I will do whatever it takes to make you and Lissa whole."

His chest heaved with some unspoken emotion. "What if that means bringing me and her back together again? What are you gonna do?"

I held his gaze, knowing I would regret it if I didn't, as I answered. "You will both forget me, soon after I leave."

"No," he argued, "Rona, I couldn't ever forget you."

"It is the way it has always been…" I began to explain.

Cain shook his head and moved so quickly I might have questioned his human status, had I not known him. I shivered as he pressed his face into the crook of my neck and rolled us so I was draped on top of him and the covers. "I'm not like the rest of them, Rona."

"I know you aren't. But I am not like anyone you have or will ever meet. I am immortal, Cain. Even if I stay with you, I do not know what would happen. Seid or the other gods could end my existence for disobeying his orders. Or maybe…" I hesitated, not knowing if I should even mention, not even begin to hope. "If the gods are merciful, I could be allowed to remain with you."

Until all of you have passed on, at least.

Cain drew me closer and sighed. "I understand if you choose to leave. If it means you get to live, I'd let you go. But you need to know, I won't ever regret a moment we've spent together."

His assurances were identical to words I had heard countless proclaim to their loves over time. Nothing in Cain's declaration was original. I had heard and seen it all and never would have expected to be swayed in such a way. But he said these things to *me*, and this made all the difference. After Cain drew me closer, if that was even possible, and began to softly sing senseless songs of love, I knew he meant it.

Guilt pressed over my shoulders, reminding me that it was my choice to choose him for now, consequences or not. This went far beyond my compulsion to test true love. Now Cain might never know how happy he could have been with Lissa.

Would anyone think less of me for following my heart?

Could I not have this small moment of happiness, until I had to let him go?

"*I was prepared to love…I understood what it was to care about someone ahead of myself. I was ready for that. When I fell in love, there was no challenge or mystery to it; love was there and ready. I never realized that I was completely unprepared to BE loved. It had never occurred to me that receiving love would change the way I breathe…*" —ANONYMOUS

20

Looking Again

When I woke the next day to the sound of rustling fabric against plastic, I knew something was wrong. Cain preferred to watch me wake up and hold me until he was called into work each day. I frowned as I dropped my legs over the edge of his bed and stood to follow the mysterious sound.

In the living room, I was greeted by the smell of freshly cooked eggs and bacon. The antique stereo, identical to the one in his uncle's flat, was on and playing a melancholy tune of soft, breathy vocals. Bent over next to the frail coat rack was Cain. His black hair was still in its naturally wild state, with tuffs sticking up in conflicting directions. As usual, he wore a thin white shirt and sleeping pants. But I was surprised to see the upturned sacks at his knees and wrapped my arms around my chest as I approached.

The wind howled beyond the brick walls of the apartment.

I thought of reaching out with my power to inspect the weather and then thought better of it. Using my abilities for leisure was not wise when the curse had been retaliating. I didn't know who was watching, Seid or worse. And judging from yesterday's attacks, *someone* was. I needed to be careful now more than ever before.

For their sake, Orona, or for yours?

Mrs. Nguyen's purchased gifts had been tossed inside the apartment the other night and left in their bags. Grateful as I was for her generosity, I hadn't given much thought to them. Cain must have seen the bags and remembered.

I reached up to hide my smile behind my fingers when I saw him pull out lacy and shimmering fabrics, undergarments and dresses. He muttered under his breath as he moved them from one pile to another then froze on a blood-colored dress.

He reached up to grasp his head with his free hand and whispered, "—crazy old bat trying to kill me?"

"Why would a bat try to kill you?" I asked, genuinely curious.

Cain jumped and twisted around so quickly he nearly lost his balance. I laughed aloud when he fell onto his backside. Cain grimaced and held up the red dress like it offended him. The lines about his eyes smoothed, however, when I crossed my legs beneath me and joined him among the piles.

"What are you doing?" I asked while resting a hand on his knee.

Cain's mouth opened and closed. His eyes shifted back and forth between the piles of clothing and me, like an animal caught in a trap. Finally, he held up the red dress Mrs. Nguyen had made me try on and traded paper for. "Finding something to wear for tonight." He waggled his eyebrows at me suggestively.

I laughed when he held the dress to his chest and posed. "Cain, those were not meant for you," I protested and reached to claw it away from him.

He easily dodged me. "You sure about that? I think this is more my color than yours, babe."

"Cain, please do not wear that. Mrs. Nguyen traded a lot of green paper for that one!" I stood on my knees to grip his broad shoulders.

His composure finally broke then, and a brilliant grin nearly split his face in two. "Well you sure ain't wearing *this* to the club tonight, no matter how much she spent. Those assholes were salivating all over my girl last time. *I'm* the only one who gets to look at you like that," he said with a wink.

Keeping a frown on my face was hard when his aura was filled with such joy. I sank back and crossed my arms over my chest for emphasis. "What do you propose then?"

After scooting back to better display his work, he held up a finger. "Before you judge me, try and see this from my perspective. I'm a slightly stronger-than-average dude, granted. But I've also got this really hot and sexy girlfriend, and while I'm appreciative of that fact, it also makes me a little bit paranoid." He stuck his tongue slightly out the corner of his mouth while digging through the nearest pile in a childlike manner. "Which is why I bring you Exhibit A."

The dress he held up before my eyes was one of my few contributions to Mrs. Nguyen's purchases. I had picked out the blue color once she approved the style. The neck scooped down, though not quite as dangerously as the garments piled together in the untouched heap.

I touched the silky fabric and smiled. "I love this one. But I am confused. Why are you so worried?"

He threw up his hands and the dress in the process. "She doesn't even know… Didn't that woman pick at least one decent getup? I've been going through all these clothes, trying to find something that isn't going to distract me on stage."

I scrunched my nose when he fingered his mother's shawl and threatened to wrap me up in that instead. But then I remembered everything he had said and all that was left unsaid. Hope and dread filled me as I asked, "On stage? Are you…did you…"

Cain shrugged as he reached for another sack and dug to reach the bottom. "I may have called Jude earlier and told him to sign me up."

"What about your work at the site?"

His gaze traveled over me in a way that made me strangely self-conscious. My fingers began to tug at the tattered hem of one of his old tee shirts. Mrs. Nguyen had insisted on buying me many undergarments, but I was fond of Cain's holy concert tees, as he called them.

"They don't need me today," he said. "We're going to the club early to practice. I haven't written much lately, so I'm going to wing it mainly and see what happens tonight."

His search at the bottom of the last bag halted when I heard the brush of fabric against plastic. Lifting a quizzical eyebrow, he tore his gaze from me and looked at the fabric he had just pulled out. The underlining of the dress was a smoky purple, the same as the skies after a storm, and draped with other sheer and glittering fabrics.

Cain shifted to his knees and leaned forward to drape it across me, his sea-blue eyes a smoldering gray. "What about this one?"

"I like it." I closed the space between us to kiss him.

His features seemed so young when I pulled back to assess them. It was then I think I realized the truth I had been pushing aside for days now. Cain was still a boy in so many ways, in spite of all he had been through. Since he wore Seid's face, I had been able to ignore this fact.

Because part of you wanted it to be him.

Unshed tears stung behind my eyes as I silently agreed.

Cain didn't ask after my tears. He only pulled me in closer, messing his separate piles as he lifted me into his lap. He deepened our kiss until I wanted to lose myself in the person I was before we had met, to be an unfeeling and unchanging immortal.

Perhaps Cain felt the change in me, because for a few moments, he simply held me and kissed my tears away.

A better person would have let him go long ago and let him forget. Or perhaps they would have taken their chance at happiness and held on to him just as fiercely? My arms squeezed reflexively around his waist, and I pulled out of our kiss to bury my face into his solidity. As I listened to his heart race and slow, he breathed me in.

"Rona, you okay, babe?" he asked with a heavy sigh.

I squeezed my eyes shut, wanting the silence, wanting to hold onto him just a little bit longer.

Let me keep you always.

"Rona?" Reaching up, he pulled my chin gently from his chest and up to meet his blue gaze.

I almost cried to see his vulnerability and his tenderness. "I am just—happy that you are playing tonight."

"Good. I'm only doing this for you." Cain's mouth drew into a pensive frown that pulled the scar on his face into a cruel angle. "I hope you're not worried about me and Lissa anymore." His eyes pursued mine vainly as he searched for any hidden truths.

He was closer to the truth than he knew. Not only was I worried for that reason, but I almost spoke a lie. I was forbidden to lie, and as far as I was aware, it was physically impossible for me to utter half-truths.

When I did not answer, Cain continued, "You think I'm gonna pretend you haven't seriously thought about splitting?" His mood changed swiftly with his words. "I know you aren't so sure about us." His voice cracked slightly, and he breathed deeply before continuing, "But I think you have to start trusting people sometime, Rona."

I reached up and pressed my fingers to the skin just above the collar of his shirt and whispered, "I *do* trust you, Cain."

"Then trust me when I say you may be some kind of goddess, but when it comes to this, I know best. I know that you were like a ghost when I first found you, but now you feel. I know you think about everyone before yourself, and that's why we're in this hole together. And even though I know there's so much you haven't and probably won't ever tell me, I love *you*."

I didn't know I was crying until he pulled me closer and

kissed my tears away. I was frozen in his arms, afraid to speak and break the spell of his affection. I knew what he needed to hear, what I confessed only once while he was awake. How I wished I could lie and promise I would never leave. Knowing the consequences, I might have still told him how deeply I loved him, in a way neither one of us could forget.

His lips pressed to mine gently, and immediately I felt the pull in my lower chest, that forbidden string attaching my body to his. With all the strength I possessed, I pushed away from Cain's arms. My body protested and my soul screamed madly, demanding I return to the only embrace I would ever want again.

Neither of us interrupted the awkward silence that followed. I fought back the sobs threatening to spill from my lips. When I glanced up at Cain, I saw how he watched the rise and fall of my chest with brooding intensity, how his fists clenched and unclenched. Colors broke out over our heads, his aura as black as a storm cloud and rolling with sparks of lightning. Cain's emotions pulsed around his frame in a wild frenzy, while outwardly he remained calm.

I shook my head as I began to put my new clothes back into the sacks. "I think I'll wear the purple dress tonight. I can ask Mrs. Nguyen to dress me again, and we can walk together. Is that okay?" I turned when Cain did not answer, and frowned.

He had already stood and walked across the room.

I numbly watched as his bedroom door shut with a light click. Only then did I give in to despair. This time it had nothing to do with Seid or my father or the man my father chose for me. It had nothing to do with the choices I had made two thousand years ago. I knew I was hurting Cain by loving him, and somehow, this new pain was the one that struck deepest.

ᔉᔉᔉ

Mrs. Nguyen answered her door after the second knock.

I carried nothing with me but the purple dress, undergarments, and heels.

Mrs. Nguyen was already in a black silk dress, draped in a cloak of shimmering gold fabric. It hugged the curves she still possessed, despite her old age. Her black-and-gray-streaked hair was piled high on top of her head in weaves that reminded me of the mother I vaguely remembered.

Her red-painted lips parted over her black-stemmed cigarette, and cherry-scented smoke escaped with her words. "Sugar, you look terrible. Come on in. Why you crying? Was it Cain? I swear if that son of a—"

"Mrs. Nguyen," I interrupted, "it is I who has wronged him." I waited until she had shut the door and locked it behind us.

For a long moment she appraised me with narrowed eyes, puffs of smoke filling the space between us.

"I hurt him. All I do is hurt him," I ground out in the end and dug my nails into my palm.

Mrs. Nguyen waved the cloud of smoke away from her face and strode forward until I could see every one of her beautiful wrinkles. "Can I give you a piece of advice, sugar?"

I nodded my assent, and she lifted one of my clenched palms with her free hand. With gentle pressure, she relaxed my tense digits and patted my skin.

"First," she said, "let's fix that gorgeous face of yours."

I waited impatiently as she sat me down on the seat before her many beauty products. After stubbing out her cigarette, she washed my face. Between hard looks and hidden smiles, she applied black kohl around the rims of my eyes. She almost spoke while curling my eyelashes with a sticky black substance.

Finally, while lining my lips, she began, "Sugar, it's clear you ain't had much time to be around these humans you claim you've helped. My advice? Stop overthinking things. Listen to Cain. Help them, sure, but stop holding yourself back. You never know what could happen if you let it."

She finished applying paste to my lips and began braiding my curls next. I watched our reflection in the mirror and smiled as her fingers combed through my hair. I smiled at the lines between her brows as she concentrated on creating perfection.

"You saw what happened to me yesterday morning," I said. "You know that I am not human. What you do not know is *why* I am no longer human. I may not be able to stay with him. If I choose to remain here, I may die, but the thought of leaving him…I—I don't know if I can do this anymore," I confessed between strained breaths.

Her black eyes snapped to mine, and to my surprise, she cackled. "Good! Glad you got that off your chest. Maybe now you won't think so hard."

At last I studied my own reflection and hardly recognized the painted and frightened-looking woman in front of me.

"You need to go check on your boy as soon as I'm finished with you. You gonna wear that dress tonight, huh? Good choice."

I squeezed the soft fabric in my hands and frowned at the

bunched smoky indigo pooling from them. "We're going to rehearsal soon. Cain's going to play his instrument tonight."

"You." Mrs. Nguyen's hands froze above me, and I lifted my gaze to find her staring at me in shock. "*You* convinced our poor boy to play?"

I already knew Cain had not played in years. But judging from her look, this was even more significant than I understood.

"Yes," I hesitantly replied. I gasped when she came from behind and grasped my hands in hers. My dress spilled over my bare legs.

Her sudden smile brightened my dark mood. "Good!" she said with a fond pat of my wrist. "I knew you were good for him! I knew you could do what she never could."

I shook my head and pulled my hands out of her grasp. Clutching my dress in my hands, I stood and walked away.

Mrs. Nguyen only knew a piece of the truth. She had seen the almost human Orona, who was orphaned and alone in the world, a woman that Cain plucked off the streets and fell in love with. What she didn't see was the undead creature Cain barely knew, the foolish human girl who fell in love with the caretaker of the seas. She hadn't seen me stand up against a hurricane or keep a cave from crushing two lovers to death. She hadn't seen me throw myself over the ones who would have turned to ashes when the volcano erupted, or made water appear from the sands to the dying in the desert. She did not know I was both savior and destroyer to so many souls.

And so I cringed when Mrs. Nguyen called after me with another cackle, "See you later, alien girl!"

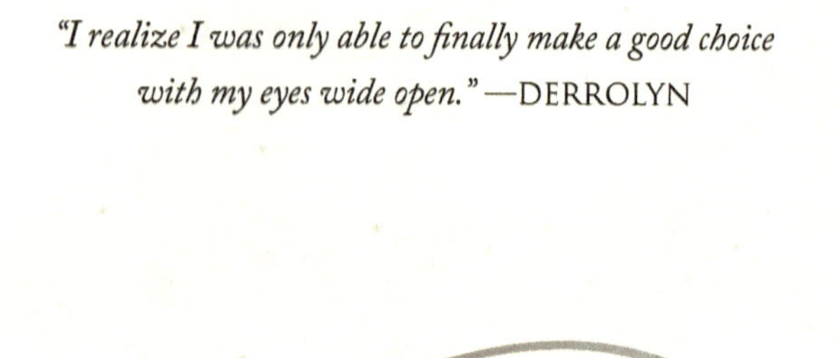

"I realize I was only able to finally make a good choice
with my eyes wide open." —DERROLYN

21

REALITY AFFIRMS

Cain adopted a convincingly carefree attitude as we rode his bike up to the club that afternoon. I savored the closeness the bike afforded us though I should have kept my distance. Instead I buried my face into the scuffed leather of his jacket, the one that smelled like the sea of his youth. I could smell myself on it from the few times he had draped it across my shoulders and the day I borrowed it to walk to the club alone. Mixed together, our scents created a heavenly brand of agony to me. I could only imagine what he felt every time I tightened my arms around his waist.

Before Cain, I had breathed in these city streets as an indifferent apparition and viewed its inhabitants like the brittle flowers they were. They bloomed and gave beauty to the world around them for such a short time before shriveling up and returning to dust. I had been disgusted with how they toyed with love amid their desperate search for fulfillment. Humans had become like a pack of starving, sniveling, smelly creatures that I wanted nothing more to do with.

How very—godlike and unworthy of me. Of course, I never considered myself like Seid, one of the beautiful, unattainable immortals, either. World-weary better described my state of mind two weeks ago.

Now, inexplicably, the roar and rumble of the engine coupled with the feel of our hearts beating together through the layers separating us made me feel alive. People *looked* at me as we passed, and they looked at Cain as he stopped before the lines of vehicles and signal lights. There was a constant rhythm to this city set by the pounding of their feet on the sidewalks. Music and voices and the screech of metal were the temporary legacy of this generation. Tonight, I was a part of it because of Cain.

He had promised he would not pressure me into anything. I believe if I had been any other girl, he would have shied away from any sort of commitment beyond occasional intimacy. But the fire between us was deeper and more dangerous than either of us anticipated. It should have frightened him, how quickly we'd settled into each other. It should have scared me more, how he wooed me with his acceptance and patience.

Can anyone truly know when love takes hold of them? And if so, who would want to prevent it? The idea of love frightened me, because every day of my existence reminded me what happened the first time I lost my heart. I saw how fragile and foolish humans were. I would have never chosen this fate for myself.

For the chance to know Cain, I would have done it again instantly, willingly.

When the bike came to a gravel-strained stop in the back alley around the side of the club, I was reluctant to let him go. Cain rested his booted feet on either side of us, and I shifted, feeling the strap that attached his instrument to me pulling at my chest. After he turned off the switch, he bowed his head and rested his hands on the handlebars. There we sat in a silence, in the muted bubble surrounding us and keeping out the rest of the world.

I drew my hands over his leather-coated back, and he shivered then sighed. "Once was enough for me, you know. I'm not mad because you won't say it back, Rona."

My nails dug slightly into his jacket as I shut my eyes against my guilt.

"Baby." He twisted in his seat to face me. With his free hand, he grasped my chin. "Please look at me."

His thumb brushed the lid of my eye. My lashes fluttered and parted as I gave in. His beauty stole my guilt and threatened my resolve as he said, "I love you. I don't care that it's been a week and none of this makes any sense. I guess I just hate being reminded that you might leave one of these days. And I hate even more the fact I could forget you. It's not like I can offer you forever. I want you to live, baby, whether that's with me or out there being Wonder Woman to lost souls."

"Cain, what are you—"

The pad of his thumb pressed to my lips as he interrupted, "Don't worry about tomorrow. Just think about today for now, for me, okay?"

This was dangerous. *He* was dangerous because what he was offering was a license to my greatest temptation. I wanted to live for the present and not think about the consequences. I would gladly endure an eternity of fire beneath my skin if it meant I could be near him, touch him. A wicked part of me rose in triumph, and I nearly agreed with him.

Instead, I remembered the reason behind tonight and forced the words I knew I would regret. "Is that what helped you recover from the loss of your baby?"

Emotion wrenched Cain's face, and he cowered from me as if I had dealt a physical blow to him. He wasted no time getting off the bike then and kicked out the metal stick to hold it in place. The love and hope in his face was replaced by a time-hardened mask.

With his lips pinched and his square jaw clenched so tightly, I almost didn't recognize him. Emotions brewed above him and around his form in black-stained shades of red. I fought back tears and hated myself for my need to push him away.

He grasped the handle of his bike and turned his shoulder away from me. The harsh line of his square jaw faced my line of sight, and his words escaped his lips. "How do you know about the baby?"

"Lissa still has not recovered from her choice."

Cain laughed bitterly, an abrasive thing, and muttered, "Exactly, *her* choice. I—I didn't know she was pregnant until—until after she decided to get rid of it…"

As he trailed off at the end, I clutched my chest with my hands to keep from wrapping my arms around him. This wasn't about me and my selfishness or these stupid, addictive human emotions any longer. It was about Cain and Lissa and their baby.

It was always about your mission, Orona.

Cain dipped his head low and looked up at me through his dark lashes. "Look, Rona, I can't do this right now. Between rehearsal and dealing with all those people in there." He must have seen something he didn't like in my expression, because he turned away. After hesitating a moment, he said, "Let's just get through the next couple of hours, and maybe later tonight I'll tell you exactly what happened between me and Lissa."

Keeping my chin safely tucked into my chest kept me from having to meet his eye. The veil my hair created also allowed me to measure his reaction when I nodded. Cain walked to the side entrance and wrenched the door open, then held it open for me. I adjusted the strap keeping his instrument secured to my back as I slinked off his bike and followed.

Cain wiped the tears welling in his eyes as I approached. I was surprised by the vehemence of his reaction, but then again, I wasn't. Cain had not just lost his child, but Lissa. Easy as it would have been for us to pretend otherwise, I knew a part of him would always carry her in his heart.

His hands brushed my shoulders as he pulled the instrument case over my head and hefted it over his shoulder. I stared at his scuffed-up black boots, at the way the sunlight bounced off the silver buckle, anything to keep from looking him in the eye.

I forced myself to remember that I was already dead, living on borrowed time. I didn't belong in this world of humans any longer. This world belonged to people like Cain and Lissa and their children.

Children you will never have.

I gasped at the unexpectedly painful thought and trudged down the stairs after him.

Music greeted us at the bottom of the stairwell, the same breathy, brassy kind I listened to every day in his apartment. Here in the club, everything was much more real. I could easily picture the young Cain and Jude scampering between tables and behind the bar where they shouldn't be.

Musicians and dancers flitted in and out of the dressing rooms half clothed, and a few of the women shrieked with embarrassment when they saw Cain. He glanced at me from the corner of his eye, and his scar creased deeper into his flesh as he grinned at me. My furrowed brow smoothed, and I smiled back. It would seem, in spite of everything, nothing had changed between us in Cain's eyes.

Stage lights were already fully honed in on the instruments and their players rehearsing for the show later tonight. Cain had told me a rough idea of the way things would go. He assumed I was dancing again, but I was unwilling to expose myself to anyone tonight. This night was about him.

Cain didn't like revealing much about himself to most people, I had learned. Apparently Jude and Lissa knew a lot more than Cain would have liked them to. Now that I knew pieces of their shared past, I understood why Cain tensed the moment they met us backstage.

Jude approached with a swaggering step and thick dollop of charisma on his tongue. "Hot damn! Never thought anyone was gonna get you back on that stage again, little cuz. She must be *really* good." His laughter was quickly cut off after a jab of

Cain's fist to his arm. Jude scowled a moment and rubbed the sore spot.

"Serves you right," Lissa drawled over him with a sneer and reluctantly met my eye. "He's got a point though. Orona must be something special to get *you* here."

Had I not heard the wistfulness in her tone, or caught the flicker of longing in her gaze as she looked to Cain, I might have thought she was jealous. Her reaction only confirmed my suspicions.

"She is." Cain wrapped his arm around my shoulders, pulling me into his warm side.

Jude laughed and arched an eyebrow. "Good thing. We were short of acts tonight. Lissa here can finally rest that gorgeous voice of hers. Ain't that right, baby?"

Lissa pasted a false smile on her face when he reached over and clasped her neck with his hand. Only I caught the flicker of pain in her green gaze. Briefly, I recalled how haggard and broken she had looked in Derek's apartment. I quickly scanned her skin for bruises to see if she had gone home with him last night after all.

Lissa's hand reached up to cover her bare arm then, hovering over the very place my eyes had been fixed on. Before I could confront her, she had turned and slipped away.

Jude called out to the instrument players, "Aw, man, now what kind of garbage is that? Am I paying you to write your own music? You expect to draw in a crowd or turn them away?"

Cain's chest expanded against mine, and I looked up at him just in time to catch his pensive study of the stage.

I squeezed his arm and pulled his attention back to me.

"You are going to do well. Remember how you told me how it felt the first time you played for your uncle?" He nodded and tucked his chin into his chest. I smiled. "This time you will play for you."

"I'd better get up there," he replied with a lift of his shoulders. The movement was just enough to pry him from my touch, and I sadly watched as he approached the stage.

Jude noticed his taller cousin and clapped a hand on his shoulder before he could pass him by. This time, Cain did not reject the teasing banter.

I slipped into the shadows and sat upon one of the many empty plush barstools. I watched as the other musicians ceased in their playing to greet Cain. He climbed upon the stage and stiffened against an onslaught of hugs and exclamations. I watched fondly, even as a fresh wave of pain clenched my chest and refused to let go.

The heart that should not be still beating clenched in a tight vise, and needle-sharp pricks danced up and down my chest.

Not now! Please!

I reached out to clasp the edge of the bar as I doubled over and struggled for breath. I *would not* ruin this for Cain. Nothing mattered more to me now than his healing. Music was the key to his soul, as the sea had once been to mine. Sound thickened and grew muffled around me.

Time blurred and rushed past me before I could catch hold.

Far too soon, the sound of laughter gave way to amplified strings being plucked on the stage. I recognized Cain's touch even now, in the heat of the curse's hold over me.

Blood escaped my lower lip where I had bit down, and the

taste was what pulled me from the haze.

I blinked, startled to see an immeasurable short span of time had already passed. I had lost control over my gifts again.

Where is Cain? Where are Jude and the others?

Colors filled my vision as I watched the dancers grace the stage. Though I knew their personalities to be crass, onstage their movement was fluid like the swirling waters of the sea. They did not dance with the same fevered intensity as my sisters and I once had. Which was just as well, judging by the reaction my dancing had pulled from the audience the other night.

Soon my gaze wandered from the bright lights pouring in harsh lines above, to the halos of color emanating over everyone's heads. Immediately I straightened and stared, disbelieving.

This is new.

Fear prickled in the back of my thoughts as I opened myself up to Seid's gift as far as I dared. I had spent much of my existence fighting his hold over me. Yet these past days, as I struggled to find my humanity again and my control wavered, my pain worsened. Was this what happened to Seid, when he dared to love a mortal?

For some time I had fought the obvious answer.

Now, as I chose to give in to the curse, my blood rushed with the full might of my power. Color prickled from beneath my skin, yearning to escape and unveil my true nature. The sudden rush of emotions and flicker of memories leaked from the people before me in a web of glowing blue strands that twisted together, until they were one roped cord that pierced and flooded me as it was meant to do. What frightened me most was not that it was overwhelming or too much.

It feels right.

Tears flowed down my cheeks, and I tore at the visible cord as I attempted to break the connection. The writhing blue threads followed me when I ran from the edges of the club and toward the dressing rooms.

Why didn't Cain come to find me before they began?

I needed to see Cain again, needed to ground myself in his presence. I needed his touch and his lips on mine to keep me human and safe.

When have you ever needed anything?

I told the voice in my head to shut up as I stumbled into the vacant women's dressing room. For a moment, the emptiness of the room made me feel like I was set adrift in the middle of a sea of loneliness. I realized then I had half expected to find Lissa here with the dancers. Perhaps Cain too.

Vaguely, I remembered them dancing—the other players and workers pausing to watch them rehearse. But this brought back the memory of emotions, the flickering images of their hopes and dreams and the almost-impossible-to-ignore *need* to fulfill those desperate desires.

I stared back at the broken woman in Lissa's mirror, and gasped when I saw how her eyes glowed with every color. Her skin, too, burst with ever-shifting ripples of pinks and blues and greens that swirled into softer violets and dusky orange. But her usually golden hair was lit from within, from root to end with a white light. The reflection of a weary goddess.

I wordlessly moaned and resisted the urge to smash the image of the very creature I had fought against for two thousand years. I backed away from the lights and the mirrors until I sank against the wall behind the entrance and buried my face in my hands. My heart beat in my chest like an unceasing drum, and the memory of Seid passed through my closed lids.

I ignored the whispers and fearful gazes coming from my sisters nearby. I was eldest, and therefore responsible for their well-being, especially after our mother's illness. I was to set the example of obedience and had struggled to fulfill my father's expectations. He lamented over having no sons to carry his fortune. I must carry the family legacy, he had said to me moments before.

I stared at my reflection in the mirror, the braids and flowers my sisters had helped arrange with mother's combs. The kohl lining my eyes brought out their almost violet shade, another one of my odd features that marked me apart from my dark-featured sisters.

I ignored their whispers now. A wedge had been driven between us that could not be undone. They had spied on us, on Seid and me, on our special place. Telling Father had been the worst of all choices they could have made. They did not know this yet. They were younger, and I sheltered them much.

Now I had no choice but to join with my newly proclaimed husband. What would Seid think? Was he watching even now? Did he know? I longed for the peace I felt in his presence, in his touch. Why did nothing make sense apart from him?

Father suddenly appeared in our rooms, and my sisters all bowed low in fear and subjection. His gaze met mine through the mirror. "Come," he said in that harsh, scathing tone he had begun to use recently. The steel behind his pale eyes might have terrified me more if I had not known the god of the seas.

I followed my father as one walking to her own funeral, my sisters trailing behind me.

I could never go to our secret place again, I told my rebellious heart. For the sake of my family, I would be a dutiful wife and help manage my husband's estate, as Mother taught me. I was doing this to save my family from certain poverty.

I would never see Seid again, for his sake.

I made him weaker, he had said, after all. Seid was not meant to be grounded but wild as the winds over the waters.

This was the only way.

If I had known my husband would be dead in less than two days' time, I never would have agreed to Father's demands. Seid's weakness had been greater than he or I knew. His love transformed him into a jealous, dangerous monster when he realized what I had done. To him, I had betrayed everything. He had already tried to save me from my father and the man to be my husband once before. He had vowed to destroy them all and held back his fury for my sake.

My husband paid with his life. I never was allowed to see my father and sisters, to learn what happened to them until much later. For many bitter years, I believed Seid had killed them as well. Until I returned to our inlet and saw my sisters' white heads and wrinkled skins.

Time softens as much as it hardens some.

I stared at my glowing hands, slicked wet by the moisture of my tears. For the first time, I saw the pieces of that day I had forgotten. I saw Seid's face in the moment after he rescued me from my husband's assault.

"Seid?" When I tried to follow him, to wrap my arms around him, I tripped and fell to my knees. Seid didn't move to help me up, and true fear lifted the hairs at my neck.

Never break a promise to a god.

"It wasn't their fault!" I pleaded, recognizing the sneer in his perfect lips. He blamed my father for what had happened, I knew. My god's wrath when angered was legendary, and when sparked, few could escape his fury.

"No more!" he growled, lifting a finger to me.

The changes began immediately. Gills broke my skin apart in tiny bloody slivers underneath his invisible touch. He had done this before to show me his home beneath the waves. Yet this time was different. This time other parts of me began to change and twist into something lighter, dangerous and powerful.

"What are you doing to me?" I rasped, clutching my chest where the pain began to concentrate and grow. "My love, please!"

Thunder rolled over our heads as he spoke. "You betrayed me."

The pain was unbearable as Seid inflicted his wrath on me with the force of his will. Those glorious blue eyes were frozen into cold and dark seas, indifferent to my screams. In all our tumultuous and tender times together, I had never believed he would use his power on me.

"I pledged myself to you!" I cried. "Why are you doing this?"

"You know why," he seethed.

"But I didn't truly betray you! You would have known if I had! Please, it is not their fault, Seid. Spare them, and punish me!"

My pain ceased, and a cruel smile transformed his features into something dangerously beautiful.

"Will you avow yourself to my will?"

"Anything."

"Cursed!" he cried in pain. His temper had always been as restless and unpredictable as the sea itself. But his words had power behind them. Too late to take it back.

"I grant you your wish to be with me always, yet not as we wanted," he said. "Now you will walk the earth and seas, to find love and protect it. The very emotion you betrayed, you are cursed to preserve at all costs. Always watch but never be seen, Orona, and never touch, lest you face my wrath. Cursed you will be evermore," he declared, "until time's end, until it is broken..."

This time I recalled his words with new ears and saw the memory through new eyes. I had forgotten how ruined he had been that day. Too late did I at last understand and regret my hardened shell of a soul.

Seid's curse was a bittersweet gift in disguise. Much like his nature, because he was fashioned from the sea and storms. And it had been my choice to remain bitter against him all this time. His many attempts to distract me over the first millennium that followed might have been about more than revenge, after all.

Their voices were so soft at first, I barely heard them.

I turned to peek through the crack in the dressing room doorway and caught a sliver of their shapes. Cain had his shoulders hunched and his head bowed. The mad state of his hair betrayed how often he had dragged his fingers through it in the last hour. I smiled affectionately at how youthful this habit had rendered the appearance of my mortal love.

Lissa had her fingers splayed and threaded together, twisted in tight angles as she spoke. "I shouldn't have thrown your relationship with her around like that. I didn't have any right to say what I said, and I'm sorry. I—I *like* Orona, even if she can be a little weird and intense sometimes. But she cares about you a lot, and I'd like to think—" She paused, lifted her green gaze to dart over his hardened features, then laughed. "This is ridiculous. I can't believe how awkward this is. It *shouldn't* be, you know?"

"Shouldn't it?" Cain lifted his head and bared his teeth at her.

Lissa flinched but tried desperately not to show it.

And the golden thread I had crossed an ocean to find the source of was pulsing brighter, thicker now. No longer as fragile as a spider's web, I could sense the underlying strength that had forged their bond, a thing of reliance and desperation that evolved into deep, passionate love.

The knowledge would have broken me not so long ago. But in the span of a week, I had been mended and come undone, so I could only wait and listen.

"Yeah." Lissa swore under her breath. "I'm not good at this, Cain. I don't know what you want me to say."

Cain lifted his clenched jaw, and his voice rose as he replied,

"If this is you giving me your apology, how about you start by telling me why you told Rona about our baby."

Lissa's hands absently rested over her flat abdomen, and her eyes welled with unshed tears. "What are you talking about? I never told her *anything*."

Cain threw up his hands with a curse. "Don't try throwing this back on me! I wasn't the one getting Rona drunk or dressing her up like a hooker! You always do this, never stopping to take the blame, Lissa. That's why you're in the mess you're in!" He took two steps toward her, his chest heaving.

Lissa choked on her words. "What are you saying?"

Cain snatched her bruised wrist and tugged up the sleeve to reveal the discolored skin. "*This* is what I'm talking about. You should have never got mixed up with Derek! I tried protecting you when you didn't want it, and now I don't think I would even if you wanted me to."

Lissa wrapped her hand around his. "Cain, you're hurting me…" she whispered.

He gasped and stumbled back a step, shaking his head to clear the dark aura over his head. His gaze softened.

My heart fell as I saw how their connection only grew instead of breaking completely.

"I should have told you about the baby before I made my choice," she whispered.

The harsh slant of his mouth eased and then quivered slightly. He looked so innocent to me then, so young. Even his voice seemed lighter as he answered her. "I wish you had."

Lissa's eyes widened, and I sensed this was the closest he had ever come to accepting her apology. "You sounded good back there, better than I remembered. I didn't know you could play like that."

Cain shifted on his feet. "Glad to hear I fooled you guys into thinking I'm a musical genius."

I glanced down at my fingers and the colored lights dancing just beneath the surface of my skin. The curse had taken hold of me before I could hear Cain's song. Now I wondered if this happened for a reason, something that transcended beyond my happiness.

Cain and Lissa's laughter meshed together like strings against the beat of drums. They complemented and separated one another. Flashes of happier memories passed along their connection to me, and I knew their laughter had been a common thing.

Once, Seid had made me laugh when we played in the water together. He hadn't been terrible and frightening, not to me. So often he'd been tender and mischievous.

And you buried this beneath your hate.

Clenching my fingers into a tight fist, I wanted to growl at the voice in my head. But perhaps now it was time to remember, time to face the truth. I peered through the door crack once more.

Fresh notes sang from the band onstage, through the hall, and echoed below. Lissa and Cain now stood together with their backs to the opposite wall, neither touching.

The cord connecting them seemed to be growing even brighter.

"Cain, I always thought you were made of something more, you know?" Lissa tentatively began. "Like you were gonna do great things one day. Maybe that was what scared me. I never thought I could live up to you. You're just so *good*."

Cain kept his head bowed low and shoved his hands in his pockets. "Derek gave you those bruises, didn't he?"

Lissa shrank into herself almost immediately. The Lissa I had come to know would have denied everything and pushed him aside.

The volume of Cain's breathless curse made even me flinch. "I'm gonna kill him!"

"Don't!" Lissa grasped his shirt in her hands.

Cain grunted something under his breath and turned to face her. His hands pulled her shoulders closer, and he bent until they were eye level. "Tell me the truth. No more lies, Lissa. Can you honestly tell me you're happy with the guy you left me for?"

"I was wrong! Okay? Happy I'm finally admitting I was wrong?" Lissa's voice shook through her reply. "I don't want that life anymore, Cain. All the fine things I thought I had to have…they're not important." She sucked in an uneven breath and dropped her hands from his chest and lifelessly to her sides. "I know I don't got any right to say this, but Rona helped me realize something lately."

"What?" Anger had fled from Cain's clenched jaw, changed the lines of his face into an expression of worry, of fear. Over their heads, the cord linking them continued to mend and weave together.

"Maybe," she whispered, "the thing I was missing was in front of me the whole time."

Cain's lips parted and his blue eyes widened as Lissa's strength crumbled. The wall she had surrounded her heart with crumbled to mortar. Her shoulders shook with sobs as her hands grasped, tightened in a desperate hold about his waist.

Cain glanced furtively in every direction then slowly wrapped his arms around her shoulders. He pressed his nose in her hair and sighed.

It should have hurt. It should have been agony, as I had been dreading.

A strange thing happened to my broken heart instead.

I saw Lissa as myself, fragile and desperate as I was two thousand years ago. And I did not want Lissa to make the same mistakes I did then.

"We married when I was twenty and have been married twelve years.
So, yes. I've been in love. Only once."
— COLLEEN

22

SWAN SONG

Never had I given much thought to my own actions. Once, I cared deeply for the fate of the lovers I had been led to test. But over time and the slow dilution of love in this world, the mission became nothing more than duty. Rather than pour my heart into helping the lovers survive their plight, I became a hardened, bitter creature.

Love had only reminded me of Seid. My gifts had become but a reminder of that curse. If I had not lost sight of my mission, if I had cared a little more for others, instead of feeling sorry for myself, could I have mended the leak? Would the world not be so miserable if I hadn't been so blind to all but my pain?

Before Lissa could enter the dressing rooms, I donned my cloak and watched her breeze past me. For the following minutes, I watched her sit before her mirror and wipe away the smudges her tears had created beneath her eyes. She smiled at her reflection and then covered her mouth to catch her sudden laugh. She sounded disbelieving, joyous, and then, just as quickly, terrified.

She shook her head and whispered, "What are you doing, chica?"

Could she have seen me when I moved to stand behind her, shimmering and glowing like the skies after a storm, she would have seen my struggle. Part of me wanted to tear off my cloak and demand her forget Cain and live with the consequences of her choices. I wanted to shout at her for leading Cain on and running to Derek, to Jude, to any man who would trade affection for gratification.

Instead I watched her carefully apply skin-colored paste again to the bruise on her left cheek, the one her tears had recently exposed. The joy faded from her eyes, to be replaced with acceptance.

Do you love him? I wanted to ask her.

A flurry of grating voices behind us announced the other dancers' arrival. They spoke of the important guests coming in but a few hours. I turned to the clock. Was it the evening already? How long had I been lost to the curse, trapped in my own mind? Again, why had Cain not come looking for me?

"Well, look who it is." A woman who seemed all legs spoke over the others. "Why am I not surprised?"

Lissa hastily finished touching up her skin paste and offered them her usual smirk. Ignoring Legs, she turned to the others. "You guys done rehearsing for the boss yet?"

Each of them offered different answers, each more ridiculous than the last. I fled their clucking chatter. In the brief times I had observed them, I believed that nothing they ever said in front of each other was genuine. Even Lissa seemed weary of them, now that I observed her with renewed eyes.

To find Cain, I simply followed the golden threads connecting him to Lissa, even at this distance. I was too afraid to look for the bond he and I shared.

It will snap and fade soon enough, I reminded myself.

Much had changed in the club during the short time I had hidden myself away. Cain's thread led toward the upstairs apartment I had visited with Lissa the other day. I had no wish to intrude on his visit with his uncle. So I clung to the back in my cloak and waited.

Before Cain, time had been one seamless, endless dream without meaning. Change inevitably came and went with the seasons. Sometimes, if I blinked the right way, I missed more than a lifetime.

The cleaners were busy making the floor and tables shine. Musicians warmed up their instruments, though I had listened to them playing long before this. Chloe, the cloak girl, took her post with another big-chested and muscled man. He had taken over Cain's job to protect the door this night. Drinks were poured nearby me, and then guests slowly filtered through the doors and to their seats.

With my cloak in place, I was once more invisible and grateful for it. The curse had grown in strength since I accepted it. So the oppressive webbing of their human emotions did not overwhelm me as it had before. Still, I watched the threads weave and tangle together in various shades, each glowing from the inside out. It was beautiful in a terrifying way. It made me tremble with feeling. The temptation to erect that tidal wave between my own emotions and them grew with the number of bodies in the room.

I blinked, hoping to break the connection for a few blessed moments. I needed to breathe, to remind myself why I was there. I needed to remember…

"—this girl you keep talking about, boy? I about kicked Lissa out the other day for not bringing her on in to meet me." An elderly man spoke from the stairs above my head.

Cain's voice answered sheepishly, "Sorry, Pops. I lost track of her earlier, but she'd love to meet you."

"Don't tell an old man what he wants to hear, Cain. Level with me. Is she a looker?" After a brief silence, his uncle chuckled.

Cain sighed. "You have no idea…"

"She's got legs a mile long, Pops!" Jude piped up, far too near my hiding place. "And wait till you hear that accent… Easy, brother, I wasn't trying to mack on your girl."

Pops only laughed harder, and Cain grunted something under his breath.

So he did miss me, after all.

Surprising as the idea was, I reminded myself of the hard truth. I knew what I had to do now.

"Rona?" Cain whispered, and I opened my eyes. Even hidden in my cloak, he could see me once again.

His uncle and Jude frowned and shared a look between them before Jude spoke up. "Yo, Cain, I already saved you a seat at Pop's table." When this was given no reply, he shuffled backward, hands in his pockets. "Okay then. Hope those meds you've taken don't screw with your performance. See you later, Pops. I gotta warm up the crowd."

Pops waited off to the side, watching us with interest as Cain approached.

I was frozen, held under that familiar azure gaze. Conflicting feelings washed over me as Cain closed the last few steps between the staircase and my shadow-filled corner. Relief filled his eyes as they swept over me.

"Why you got this old thing on again?" His fingers lifted to fiddle with the corners of my cloak. I cringed at the laughter in his voice. "Thought you didn't need to be invisible anymore."

Something was different about him, I decided as he slipped his hand around my waist. There were no shadows in his soul or hovering above his head. He was at peace.

She gave him that.

Cain's touch made the colors dancing beneath my skin recede and fade to a normal, human tone. His forehead rested against mine, and I let him draw me closer, even though the image of Lissa in his arms hours before was imprinted on my memory.

One last time, please, I begged the gods, *just this one last time.*

Cain's breath brushed my lips as he spoke low. "I'm sorry I flipped out on you earlier. I should have told you about the baby and Lissa. I just—never realized how much I wanted a kid until I realized I lost one. And I've hated her ever since for not giving me any choice in the matter. But that was no excuse for me to take it out on you." His arms tightened until our legs pressed together.

I took in a shuddering breath before replying, "You have both suffered much."

Cain smiled, and I tried to memorize the way his scar

made the corner of his mouth lift slightly and changed him from someone unapproachable to the loving soul he truly was. His hand gently clasped the back of my neck as he said, "You were right, about everything. I did need to forgive Lissa for the past, so we could have a future."

Ours or theirs?

"You gonna introduce us, boy?" Cain's uncle asked from behind him. Hidden by Cain's solid chest and the corner, I could almost forget the rest of the world. Cain kept one arm around my waist and turned me with him. Somehow he managed to slip my cloak off my shoulders and bunch the fabric into his free hand.

"Sorry, Pops. This is Rona," he said with pride.

Pops brought his cane up to take another hobbling step and looked at me from deep-set eyes. His skin was a lighter shade of brown than his son's, closer to Cain's roan shade. His black hair had nearly turned white, his face lined with wrinkles, but the slight tilt of his smile reminded me of Cain.

"So you're the beauty who's brought my boy out of hiding again?" He supported his weight on his cane while holding out a hand to me. I reached out and accepted it without question but was startled when he lifted it and briefly kissed my knuckles. "It's a pleasure to know you, Rona."

I smiled so deeply my cheeks ached. I was not used to such gentleness, had never known such kindness, even among my own family. "And I, you," I replied. "You are the one who taught Cain how to be a good man."

Pops looked past me to his nephew. "I think I might have to steal her from you after all. Sorry in advance, son."

Cain laughed and tugged me closer into his side. "Too late for that, old man. Already called dibs."

"You keep bringing up that old-man business, and I might have to prove which one of us can heat up that stage." I joined in their laughter as we made our way toward the vacant corner table.

"Alright, alright, looks like we've got a real crowd cooking up tonight, ladies and gents!" Jude announced into the metal stick, and his voice echoed through the building.

Cain leaned in to whisper, "He's using a microphone. It connects to the speakers and amplifies the sound."

I shook my head, unable to form a response that didn't betray my age in front of Pops. Yet when I glanced at the old man, I saw his eyes were once again watching me with veiled amusement. Cain chuckled, and I narrowed my eyes as he tried to mask his laughter.

Our noses brushed as he teased, "Don't mind him, he's just jealous."

"Not in front of these people." I pulled back when he playfully nipped at my lips.

Cain glanced toward the stage, and a secret grin stretched his handsome face.

"What are you smiling at?" I turned to follow the source of his distraction.

A beautiful voice poured through the microphone and out of the speakers to grace our ears. Instead of Lissa's jewel-like eyes glittering on stage, I met a familiar pair of coal-black eyes, carefully lined with age. She was dressed in the same extravagant robes she had worn as she ushered me out of the apartment earlier that morning. Except now her short black hair was shaped into a tight net cap, complete with a diamond-studded feather standing up to the side. Her ruby-red mouth smiled as she fixed her gaze to me and continued to croon.

"Mrs. Nguyen?" I held my breath when Cain leaned in to speak against my ear.

"She used to sing here regularly for years. Knew Pops long before that. She's the reason I found an apartment close by for so cheap," he explained.

I nodded and smiled as Cain's words resonated with everything I knew of his enigmatic neighbor. Her watchfulness over him and knowledge of his family's past all made sense now, and her sweet song gave me peace.

My breath caught as Cain's lips pressed to the skin just below my ear. Beneath the table, he caught my hand with his and trailed patterns over my open palm. So simple a touch should not have me trembling and willing to throw all my careful plans aside. "Have to get backstage," he spoke into my ear. "Mrs. Nguyen promised to look after you till after the show."

I frowned and turned to face him, only to feel his mouth against mine one last time. Then he was gone.

"I think I have been in love many times, with varying degrees of intensity.
Though nothing compares to the realization of "This is it. This is the one."
— KATE

23

BEING HUMAN

I recognized Derek in the crowd. He was dressed in a suit of the finest high-count threads. My father often dealt and traded in cloth in an age when it was considered an art. I still recalled the better years, when Father took me with him to inspect the latest cargo. I was better than a son, he had said in secret. Only later did I realize he said this because I would bring him even greater profits when he sold me to my husband.

Derek smelled like these men, like my father and my husband. His dark hair was slicked back, and his perfectly structured profile gleamed handsomely in the low light. He was sitting at the table beside mine, and to my horror, Lissa was draped on his arm just slightly behind him.

I could feel my skin begin to burn and threaten to burst with my fury. After everything I had done, everything I was willing to sacrifice, she was going to throw it all away?

My fingernails dug into the tablecloth, and power boiled

beneath my breaking point of control. After accepting the curse, it felt unnatural to contain it bottled up inside me, unless Cain was at my side.

"Agatha!" Pops exclaimed from beside me.

I jumped when a cool, wrinkled hand rested on my shoulder and turned to face Mrs. Nguyen's scrutiny. Somewhere in the back of my mind, I knew her song had ended and the band taken over during transition. I could not explain how I *knew* she was going to be disappointed in me. But I saw it in her glittering eyes, that other kind of knowing so few humans were capable of. This woman saw deeper than most, as I once had.

"Gregory," she answered finally without taking her gaze off me, "it's been a long time."

"Too long, honey. But I hear you've been looking after my nephew well enough. Figured I owed you one last performance before we both hit the dirt," he replied and laughed with her.

Mrs. Nguyen turned to speak with Pops, though her fingers squeezed my arm slightly before letting go. Enough to remind me she was watching.

I couldn't resist one last look to Derek's table. Lissa noticed my scrutiny this time and worried her lip before facing the stage.

"Can I get you anything, Pops?" Jude suddenly appeared at his father's side and winked at me.

While Pops was diverted, Mrs. Nguyen dragged the edge of her chair closer to mine. I pretended not to listen when she began to speak. "Did you know, once I was just like Lissa?"

I cocked an eyebrow in disbelief. Despite what she had hinted of her colorful past, I found it hard to believe.

"It's true!" she hissed, grimacing as she wheezed. "Listen."

She snatched my wrist in her vise-like grip. "I took the wrong path, and it wasn't till I met Gregg here my life took a better turn. That girl you've been glaring at has a second chance at the good things in life, just like you."

"I thought you hated her," I replied.

She shrugged and relaxed her grip before reaching in her pocket for a cigarette. "Hope you don't mind. Ain't had a smoke in three hours, and it's killing me."

I eyed the foul-smelling stick dubiously but listened in spite of the anger still rolling off me in waves. It was becoming more and more difficult to ignore the tangled web of emotions and images, the luminous connections surrounding me. And I sensed it was important to listen.

"I recognize brokenness when I see it," Mrs. Nguyen continued as she lit the white stick. Jude had returned with a fresh drink for his father and was speaking in hushed tones with him.

Mrs. Nguyen spoke over the band, without a care for who heard her then. "There's too much of it in the world, you know. Too many lost souls wandering around with no port to call home." She took a drag and eyed me speculatively. "Don't you think it'd be better to help them instead of letting them stay lost forever?"

Jude leapt out of his seat the moment the band finished, and the crowd began to clap. Mrs. Nguyen turned to Pops and shared jokes only the two of them could understand.

Jude had reappeared in front of the spotlight and began to speak. "Give another big hand for our band, folks!" He paused, and the applause echoed in my ears. "Next up, we have a real treat for you. Another returning member of our old school and my cousin, Cain Burkett."

The stage was clear, curtains dancing slightly on some unseen draft behind him as Jude disappeared from view. The instrument players had cleared out during his short speech. As the lights dimmed and the spotlight returned, Cain appeared, as though he had been sitting there all along. His instrument was clutched in his arms, pressed against his chest. Without lifting his eyes to the crowd, he strummed the strings of his instrument, and the sound amplified through the speakers to my ears.

As he played, I could almost imagine the rest of the world had faded. Lost to his music, I was once more with Cain in his apartment, when his song was ours, when he belonged to me.

Tonight he played for himself as a way to let go of his past. His smoky aura reflected the tone of his voice. Rather than listening to the words, I listened to the urgency in his fingers as they plucked the strings, the expressions crossing his face I had never seen before. Through his music, I sensed him saying goodbye to his sister Amy, his parents, and his baby. This song was his exorcism of the specters that had haunted every step of his life.

And then I realized this was never about me finding love again. It was about Cain healing from his wounds, about Lissa remembering who she truly was. My presence in their lives was meant to drive them together, not tear them further apart. My mission transcended my happiness. It was time I started living like it.

Derek's frame shifted in the corner of my vision, and I turned my head to follow his ascent. He wrapped a firm hand around Lissa's arm and pulled. Her lips twisted into a scowl, and she hissed a protest. He coaxed her with smoother touches and kisses to her neck. Her eyes drifted reluctantly to Cain one last time.

I could see it then, the cord binding them together. The rope burned so brightly that tinier threads of energy occasionally escaped and brushed the others spread across the room in a silver web. But Cain and Lissa's connection, their love for one another, was brighter. And as she followed Derek from their table and across the floor, I watched the cord stretch and rapidly begin to fade.

No! I inwardly screamed and leapt out of my seat. My limbs didn't belong to me then as I jerked the hood of my cloak over my head and let the curse fill me. My eyes fixed on Derek and Lissa's retreating backs, and I glanced at a nearby server.

I felt the familiar tug and pull of energy twisting in my gut and concentrated on the floor beneath their feet. Sure enough, the server slipped on the suddenly wet floor and the contents of their tray landed on Derek's finely tailored suit. He growled while others around them hissed and shushed him.

Distantly I heard Cain continue to play as his voice faded and Lissa moved to help Derek. Before she could touch him, I snatched her hand in mine and pulled her with me, away from her dark beloved and his weightless promises.

I glanced over my shoulder as we darted up the stairs and through the secret room, out the double doors and into the frozen city. Lissa started shouting the moment we had passed through the doors then froze as the hood fell back onto my shoulders.

"Orona? What the hell! Why did you do that?" Her wild

green eyes searched mine. She looked at me as though she had never seen me before, and this was when I caught my glowing reflection in the glass window nearby. Colors of every shade dashed rapidly across my skin.

I shook my head to dispel the image and willed her to finally hear me as I said, "You must not go with Derek!"

Lissa cursed and marched up to me until the fury of her scarlet aura clouded the space between us. "Like I said before, it's none of your business, Rona! Why can't you just let it go? I don't care what you think. I'm not good enough for anyone, but at least Derek pays the bills!"

As she finished, I watched the thread that had bound her soul to his, to Cain, sever and finally snap. The light in her emerald eyes, the brief joy I had watched take her in his embrace, dulled and faded to nothingness.

"And what about Cain?" I feebly replied.

Lissa clenched her hands into tight fists. "Shouldn't you be asking yourself that question?" With another shake of her head, she sighed. "I'm going to hail a cab." She turned to the street and the nearby hub of vehicles and traffic.

I followed, desperate to stop her, but the curse was too much a part of me now, and in this moment, I embraced it.

"Taxi!" Lissa yelled as she chased down one of the yellow-painted vehicles.

"Rona?" Cain's voice distantly called from behind me. Like a match, his voice sparked the light I had been missing, and I finally knew what I had to do.

Lissa stopped as the taxi began its approach. I picked up my feet as I unleashed the full power of Seid's curse raging inside of me. Like the tempest its maker was fashioned from, the power built and burst and merged with the ice on the street. I watched as rivulets of scarlet energy grabbed hold of the taxi's wheels and pulled at them.

A terrifying metallic screech filled our ears as the vehicle came rushing toward us. Lissa froze in horror as the headlights turned and filled our vision. I reached her just as the sickening crunch echoed loudly against our bodies, as the front of the car gave way and drove into the nearby pole.

My arms held Lissa in place as I took the full brunt of the impact. Our eyes met, and the truth of what I was faced her. Lissa screamed until she passed from consciousness. I knew she would not remember this moment later.

But something was wrong. This pain was as bad as the day Seid cursed my body into something immortal, unnatural.

Lissa needed to survive, and so I held onto her and lifted my head as we hit the ice-coated concrete.

The club's entrance blurred and then refocused as other figures emerged from within. Cain rushed ahead of them, shouting and screaming unintelligibly. I wanted to draw up the hood of my cloak and let him forget me at last, to push this behind me as a sweet and terrible dream. Instead the pain gave way to a cold numbness, the same I had lived with for an age.

I was fading and so released Lissa, crawled away from her body with broken and torn limbs. A thick, hot wetness spilled underneath me, and for the first time in two thousand years, knew I was fully human again.

Seid's words haunted me, *"Cursed you will be evermore, until time's end, until it is broken…"*

I stretched my arm and rested my cheek against it, marveling at the oddity of feeling so much. Every breath seemed to rip my insides apart again. The urge to sleep was overwhelmingly powerful. The last thing I heard was Cain screaming Lissa's name, and then there was nothing but empty weightlessness.

ᔕᔕᔕ

Floating in that endless sea of peaceful blackness was not as terrifying as I had imagined as a child. Instead, I felt secure and *full* of the things I had been missing all my time under the curse. Of all the things I could have done, allowing the emptiness to carry me on forever, to the next port, I chose to remember Cain.

We watched the snow fall again from the warm safety of his apartment. His arms were wrapped securely around me, and he broke the long silence to speak when he thought I wasn't listening, "Having you in my life is enough."

Perhaps it was this memory of his voice that made me return to the land of the living. Maybe I never left it to begin with. All I know is I woke up hearing his voice.

"C'mon, please don't leave, baby," he begged. "Please…"

I opened my eyes to find the pain in my body had receded. I was still lying alone in my own blood, my cheek pressed to my stretched arm.

Cain had Lissa cradled in his arms, his words whispered over her in a silent prayer of tears.

He doesn't see me.

My heart broke for the second time, and I wanted to die then, to return to the blackness. And then I felt it, that tug and flicker of something else burrowed deep inside me, Seid's imprint on my soul.

Why can you not leave me to die in peace? I silently asked him. I had broken the curse, but why did I feel the stirrings of power anew?

A sob escaped my lips, and I held in my sorrow as I watched Lissa open her eyes and wrap her arms around Cain's neck. He clung to her like life itself, and neither of them turned to face me. Other lights and vehicles and people had arrived since I came back to life. None of them glanced my way or followed the trail of my blood.

I wondered how I was alive, besides the possibility of Seid's sick and twisted idea of a joke. Truly I wanted to think the worst of him.

But what if he wants you to live, not to punish you, but because he cannot bear to let you go?

A sense of fulfillment washed over me as I watched Lissa and Cain embrace. I knew they would live long and happy lives together. Eventually, they would answer, when others asked how she survived the crash, that they could not remember. They would push the memory of me away until it was nothing more than a vague dream. Perhaps it was for the best they remain ignorant of a hidden world they can never see. I have never been able to forget their faces, the ones I managed to save and failed.

But for this last time, I knew I had passed the test given to me. I had chosen life for them. So, too, in that moment I realized I was no longer bleeding. My body was no longer numb but more vibrant and alive than I had felt since those stolen hours in Cain's arms.

I stood on slightly unsteady feet and smiled faintly at the crowd of onlookers. Everyone watched as Cain helped Lissa walk to a small crew of uniformed men. And my eyes flickered then connected with a pair of coal-black eyes that saw farther than most humans. Mrs. Nguyen smiled, and I nodded to her before turning my back on the club and the people who call it home.

"Love is ever changing, just like us. Sometimes it's good and sometimes it's not so good, but in the end, if you have each other to lean on, you can keep the love growing, and not just love them, but keep being in love with them."
—BETH

Epilogue

I wasn't sure what I was now, immortal or mortal, human or something more. In the end, none of it seemed to matter anymore. In the past, I had always been called somewhere, pulled every which way around the earth. For once I was alone, and it was my choice, by my terms.

I stared out at the sea, away from human eyes and the modern blemishes that covered the ruins of my people's culture. Standing in the very place we had stood all those years ago, preserved miraculously for reasons I didn't know, I could see it so clearly. I remembered the moment that Seid cursed me, binding me to him in a way far different from what I imagined. How could our love have become so twisted, so wrong?

For the first time in millennia, I allowed my tears to flow for him, for us, and the way we loved. I had not seen him for ages, but I could never forget. I had been tested by the human who wore his face for a time, to awaken me to the truth.

At least Cain and Lissa had found each other again. I prayed they endeavored to deserve each other. Impossible as I found it to comprehend, my heart still ached to think of my human. I gave Cain up because I had finally been brave enough to make the better, harder choice. I wasn't going to cause others to suffer for my joy, or run away from love because I was too afraid. My time had passed ages ago. My place was here, by the sea, and little as I cared to own to it, with *him*, wherever Seid was.

Clouds rolled over a sea so green I shivered to see its beauty once more. There was a reason I never came here. Now that I had this newfound freedom, I was uncertain where to go next. My heart told me to come here, where it all began and where it must end.

"Seid…" I whispered, my words instantly captured by a gust of strong sea air. My hair pulled against the wind, rolling in waves before me. I closed my eyes when the rain began. Moments before, the skies had been clear. The storm should not have come so quickly, yet I was not the source of this change.

My nerves stood on a thousand ends, the rain like a cool kiss, washing away my tears and my pain. I felt the piercing presence of eyes upon my back, tracing my fragile frame. My heart began to race and pound loudly in my ears, and I turned slowly, deliberately. The wind whipped my curls up and over my head, so powerfully it was nearly impossible to see.

For a moment I told myself this was a dream, an apparition of the mind. Those cerulean eyes could not belong to my one true love. His skin was as dark as the storm, once more. Only this time, the lightning that traced patterns over his skin was because of a different emotion. He bore the same face that had been planted on my human, but this was where their similarities ended. Seid's eyes were ageless. His close-cropped black hair looked surreal, like a wisp of smoke, and his chest was bare of all markings.

He moved with a graceful ease that most men could never try to possess.

I gasped and breathed shallowly, waiting, hating myself for wanting things I had already turned my back on long ago.

He leaned as though to step closer then hesitated. "You *left*," he said at last in his voice that sounded so foreign and yet belonged to no people.

I gasped, not expecting his answer, dreading and hoping as he took two more strides. Only these last steps and he was standing before me, illuminated by the setting sun and pale moon. The golden glow cast on his dark skin made his strong features more pronounced. I felt as though I was drowning, not because of his imperfect beauty, but because of the indecision in his eyes.

A small smile quirked at his lips, and he said, "Did you know, the first time I saw you, it was like waking from a dream, or maybe falling into one instead. I knew that I knew you, Rona, even though we had never met before."

I exhaled the breath I hadn't known I had been holding when he reached out and began to twist a stray curl between his fingers. He laughed bitterly, and I didn't know whether to laugh or cry, whether he was about to take me in his arms or cast me off forever.

Gulping down another breath, I frowned, puzzled by his vague explanation. "I do not understand."

With a wry twist of his mouth, he released my blond tresses and replied, "Of course you do. It's been so obvious all along, but you were too afraid to see it. Can you honestly tell me that you didn't know the truth, from the moment you saw Cain? The moment you watched me *see* you? Why else did you think he was able to see through my own invention?" he said while fingering the silken edge of my cloak.

My lips parted and shaped into a silent "oh."

His eyes crinkled at the corners, yet the expression on his face was anything but lighthearted. In fact, he looked poised to pounce on me, leaning so close into my personal space. I couldn't just see, but could actually feel how much he wanted to grab me.

"I still don't remember everything…" he began heavily, "but I think I cursed myself when I realized you could never forgive me again." His voice cracked, and storms began to brew in his gaze. We both sucked in a sharp breath when he lifted a hand and let it hover just over my jaw. "I think I remember waking up one day as a child by the sea and still craving the way you made me more at peace than anything I have ever known."

I closed my eyes when his hand *did* alight onto my cheek, when his thumb reached up to rub against my tears. Breathing was becoming more difficult. Silence seemed to be the only response I could give him, when inside my soul was raging.

"But I started to forget, the longer I was human. That was my curse, being forced to forget you." His words were still tortured and strained, not quite tender as I received them. Nonetheless, I savored every syllable, every nuance of every phrase.

"I do not remember how many lifetimes I have lived with this face, always in a different place, sharing a different human body. Every time I began to remember who I was before, I tried to take back the power. I would fail my own test and be forced to begin anew," he growled, and lightning struck the waves, illuminating the depths below.

My eyes opened in shock when he pressed his forehead to mine, and the air was stolen from my chest. Tempests brewed just behind his gaze, as ancient and fathomless as the deep, as the waves. His lips brushed against mine as he said, "But then I woke up inside *him* one day and knew it was different. I could feel you were close, my love. Even sharing his time with you, forcing what little I could of myself into him, was worth it."

He paused, considering his words. "You wanted Cain to forgive Lissa for not being the woman he was waiting for. You wanted his happiness above your own and were willing to let him go, even after you forgave me."

He wanted to hear the words from me. He wanted to know that I still desired not just Cain, but *all of him*. The unspoken question was in his words and in the eyes boring into mine, reflecting flashes of lightning.

A question that demanded an answer I was too shocked and dumbfounded to give but floated at the tip of my tongue. The feeble words I wanted to tell him died at my lips and crumpled to dust in my mind. After all, when the impossible had become possible, when my sorrow had turned into a foreign joy bubbling up in me, there was nothing left to say.

So I shifted my lower body and aligned it with his, until we were crushed together and all distance had been removed. Tentatively, I dragged a hand up through his scalp and grasped at the black, almost intangible silken hair—Seid's hair. I breathed in his air, and my chest shook with silent sobs as the enormity of all he had said, of everything that had been done and forgiven, resounded in my mind.

"You cursed yourself for me," I whispered, and almost instantly, the brewing hurricane ceased around us. My skin glowed with the presence of every color, of the sun, when he lifted his hands and pressed the tips of his fingers to my face.

A surge of longing filled me, deep as has ever been felt by two split by jealousy and pride. Because of Cain and Lissa, I had learned how to forgive Seid. I know he saw my answer in my eyes as he picked me up by the waist and crushed me to him. The moment our lips met, I could taste the truth a dozen words could never convey, but we did not question our second chance. Most people never live to discover their first.

Acknowledgements

I started writing this novel as a short story. Later, while suffering through writer's block while working on Silver Hollow, Stay became a way for me to vent some creative juices. As part of my research, I interviewed dozens of women in and beyond my acquaintance, asking them to share with me the story of their true loves.

What was born of their stories took me by surprise. I don't think this is the greatest love story ever told. It's more a tale of discovery, of things once lost and now found. Stay was written as an answer to my own question, whether or not true love exists, and if so, how far people are willing to go for it.

So thank you to all the brave women who shared their stories with me. Y'all are the reason this book was made possible. I only wish everyone could hear your mostly heartwarming and at times wrenching tales.

Many thanks to my brilliant editor, R.J Locksley, for her insight. To Bethany, Sandy, and Allison, for listening to and reading those early drafts. And much love to my designers, Najla Qamber (a.k.a. Batman), and Nada Qamber (Nevermore) for their unwavering love and support.

If you enjoyed Stay, please show your support through reviews and posts. Keep reading for an exclusive peek at the sequel, Fade. Happy reading!

ᕙᕗᕙᕗ

(Cursed Gods #2)

T hey'd been shouting at one another for nearly an hour now. Or rather, the old man had offered his exact opinion of me and my father's obvious influence.

"—can't pretend like she's one of them, Rona!"

I rested my chin on my bare knees and dug my toes and fingers deeper into the sand. I had come to the shoreline to watch the tide bring in the sunset, and to vainly try to drown out their argument. Being human might have been nice just then.

"I am not asking you to pretend, Cain… I just—" my mother sputtered, only to be interrupted.

"Remember how well your pretending worked out last time, Rona?"

"You were not supposed to remember!" Mother rarely lost her temper or control. It was why she balanced my father and I so well. Her shout silenced Mr. Burkett, at least.

Good…have to put up with that old fossil daily already.

The water toyed with me, rolling up so it almost touched my feet. I grinned at the distant rain clouds gathering in the distance. A part of me wanted to run across the waves until I found my father in the crux of the storm. He would gladly let me join the winds. He was the one who thought Mother's idea ridiculous.

"Philomena is not a human child. Why must we punish her?"

"Let her learn before she makes our mistakes, Seid."

I glanced back over my shoulder and scowled at the open cottage doorway. Mother literally lit up the usually dark and grimy interior. It was amusing to watch her glitter effect not impact a human. Not for the first time, I wondered exactly how Mr. Burkett knew my mother and father. My parents were not exactly the type to keep mortal friends. Part of the old rule was to keep away from humans, and the others seemed happy enough to do just that, except for her. All Mother said before dropping me on his doorstep was, "Cain is a dear friend, Aella."

Judging from the way the old man slammed his front door in her face, I doubted he felt the same way.

For a long amusing moment, Mother stood with her back to me and her face in the narrow space between the salt-blasted wood.

I shook my head and chose to face the sea instead. I blinked, and not surprisingly, she was already sitting in the sand at my side. Color pulsed through and around her, and I observed how it seemed hesitant of my brown skin. Our gifts didn't mesh any easier than our personalities.

I gave her a moment to rip into me again and then offered, "Well, this is familiar."

She didn't laugh, and I couldn't help but to smirk at her a little. After all, what child doesn't like seeing their parents unhinged once in a while?

"Do you mean dealing with your loss of control in front of humans?" she hissed. "Or do you speak of Cain?"

I winced in spite of myself. One thing I hated was being reminded that I wasn't in control. But it had never been a problem to my parents until this past year, when I turned forty.

"He does like to yell at you, and me, you know," I said. "All that human ever tells me is to clean, and pick up clothes, and do my homework. Don't get me started on what I'm not allowed to touch in that house. Is this what their offspring usually go through? If so, I understand why Father hated being human."

Mother didn't like it when I complained.

"Your father hated being human because he was never meant to live in human skin. But I was born human, and there is a part of you, whether you choose to admit it, Aella, that misses it too."

I couldn't help rolling my eyes at that old argument. "You can't miss something you never had, Mother. Are we done with this lecture? I want to go home. I miss Father and the sea. I'm sick of high school, and this cottage, and *that man*."

"You have only been here two weeks. Three months are what we agreed upon, Aella."

I turned my head to avoid the warning in her rainbow-colored eyes and traced patterns in the sand. "I know," I muttered. "It's just…"

I didn't want to admit it, couldn't tell her the truth. A shifting of colors was my only warning before she knelt in front of me. Anyone sitting face-to-face with my mother would have difficulty looking away too.

"What is it, little pearl?"

I cringed at the endearment. If I hadn't felt childish and weak before, I did now. Emotions bubbled up inside me, and I pressed my hands into the sand in case the sparks began again. I forced a hardness into my voice. "Every day the humans go through the same motions. Most of them don't even try to find meaning in this existence." I thought of the way the cruel boys taunted the plain girl in my class and her sob when the glasses cut her face as she fell.

"They're sad, wicked, and diseased, and I hate them!" I hung my head and shut my eyes, wishing this could all disappear, that one of my kind would interfere and take me away. There had to be an easier way to learn to control my powers than *this*.

Mother's hand rested over mine, and her voice blurred with the brush of waves on the shore. "Never forget, Aella, even the most helpless and darkest souls deserve a chance to find the light."

I looked up only to find Mother already faded, moonlight casting a silver glaze in her place over the calm port. "Typical," I snorted, "run away from another argument."

"Aella!" Mr. Burkett shouted from the white-washed cottage door.

Like the paint, Mother's friend was weathered to a blurred reflection of who he used to be. I'd seen the photos of him and his wife, Lissa. There was a time when they were what some might call handsome.

"Don't make me come after you, child!" he threatened before pausing to catch his breath.

I rolled my eyes and cast a lingering glance at the horizon. I longed to chase the sun and the storm. Instead I turned around and followed the warm light up the steps to the beach house.

About the Author

Jennifer Silverwood has been involved in the publishing world since 2012 and is passionate about supporting the writing community however she can. After studying traditional art at University, she began helping Qamber Designs & Media bring authors' books to life. Jennifer is the founder of We Write Fantasy, a blog and support group for fellow genre authors. She is the author of three series—Wylder Tales, Seven Deadly Sins, and the Borderlands Saga—and the romance titles Stay and She Walks in Moonlight.

Discover more about the Cursed Gods Series, along with Jennifer's blog on writing life and other bookish delights at www.jennifersilverwood.com